Day of the Buzzard

**Center Point
Large Print**

**This Large Print Book carries the
Seal of Approval of N.A.V.H.**

Day of the Buzzard

T.V. OLSEN

CENTER POINT PUBLISHING
THORNDIKE, MAINE

This Center Point Large Print edition
is published in the year 2007 by arrangement with
Golden West Literary Agency.

The text of this Large Print edition is unabridged. In other
aspects, this book may vary from the original edition. Printed in
Thailand. Set in 16-point Times New Roman type.

ISBN-10: 1-58547-947-0
ISBN-13: 978-1-58547-947-4

Cataloging-in-Publication data is available from the Library of Congress.

Day of the Buzzard

I

The two riders came into Corazon at mid-afternoon. Both of them were exhausted, sweated and punished by hours and miles of heat that shimmered in distorting waves off the desert floor. They rode warily, eyes squinted against the slant of sun, their rifles held ready to hand across their pommels, Corazon wasn't much. Squatting like a neutral-colored cur against a red-tan rollaway of scorched flats, it consisted of one rambling 'dobe building built in three sections: dwelling, general store, swing station for the Largo and Lansing Stage Company.

The two men had seen the spiral of oily black smoke an hour back; minutes ago they'd marked the static winged dots that were buzzards circling above the smoking ruin. When they were still yards from the station, the men hauled rein and took in the scene carefully. The sun-baked walls were standing, but the roof had burned and collapsed, a tangle of blackened timbers and charred rubble that continued to smolder fitfully. Off behind the station stood a mud-walled stable with a corral of ocotillo poles. Both were empty, the stable doors gaping open, one side of the corral broken down. Trampled earth showed that the livestock had been driven off in a body.

Dismounting stiffly and cautiously, the pair approached the main building. Angry clouds of flies swirled up. The older man's flint-cold gaze appraised

7

everything. His young companion had eyes for nothing but the three dead bodies. The flies settled again; their dim droning ebbed into a brassy wash of silence.

The older man broke it. "Our men been here sure. Track says so. But they didn't do this."

"Apaches?"

"Sure, 'Paches. Cherry-cow work, Cayetano's bunch. Wouldn't be no others."

Jason's throat muscles worked. Staring at the bodies, he fought to keep from being sick then and there. One of the men, an old Mexican, lay in the dust by the corral, his calico shirt and trousers clotted with dark stains. A hayfork stood upright in his chest, the tines driven clean through his body. He must have been shot several times, dead before the fork was thrust in; little bleeding showed around the tines. The hot wind stirred his gray hair. The woman's body lay half in, half out of the station door, her clothes and hair burned away. A Mexican too, probably in her middle years. Few of the details of sex or race or age had survived the terrible butchery, and they no longer mattered.

The worst of it had been inflicted on the third Mexican. A rope had been slung around his ankles and flung over the limb of a lone cottonwood, his body yanked upside down a couple feet off the ground, and the rope lashed down. Then a fire had been built under his head. The buzzards had been at all three bodies.

The older man followed the direction of Jason's gaze and said in that flat, chill, stolid voice that the youth was learning to hate, "You boil a man's brains in his

8

skull a spell, they just naturally bust out. One thing, 'Paches don't lift hair. You got to say that for 'em." He spat into the dust. "Leave that to the Mexes. Greaser governors down in Chihuahua and Sonora got a bounty on 'Pache scalps."

"God, Mr. Penmark." Jason's jaws were clamped; he gritted out the words.

"God ain't got a whit to do with it, boy."

Penmark turned away, a tall, gaunt and weather-worn man whose wide shoulders strained his hickory shirt. He was in his mid-fifties, but it hardly showed except in the piebald streaking of his hair and the deep grooves in his saddle-brown face. Nearly three decades of coping with this land on its own terms had made Val Penmark tough as rawhide, beating every shred of softness out of him. His nose curved like a hawk's beak. The eyes, socketed deep below his dust-powdered brows, glimmered like pond ice, dead and cold.

Tucking his Winchester under his arm, the muzzle slacked downward, Penmark studied the ground.

"Been a time. Happened, I'd say, before noon." He flicked a glance at the carrion birds wheeling on the tarnished sky. "Time enough for them to get in some work. Not too much. Our men coming here would of interrupted 'em. That'd be 'bout an hour ago."

Jason, unable to tear his eyes from the bodies, hardly heard him. Stories heard in his Missouri boyhood, tales of bloodletting and massacre told by a grandfather who had fought the Creeks and Seminoles with Andy Jackson, flashed across his memory with a raw force;

9

and suddenly, in the blistering heat of mid-afternoon, he shuddered with a sweepback of childhood fears. Abruptly the roiling in his guts surged bitter-hot to his throat. Stumbling a distance away, he bent over and threw up every particle in his stomach.

While Jason was still feebly retching, Penmark said in his flat and indifferent voice, "Time we got moving. Our men been here and gone. We are closing distance. Good chance we can come up on 'em before sundown."

"Mr. Penmark—" Jason swallowed a couple times and looked up, blinking. "We got to bury these people. Take time for that anyways."

Val Penmark's mouth was a tight slash in his granite jaw; it gave a dry twitch that was no smile. "You can't even bear the looking, Drum. You got the belly for burying?"

"Yes. It's the Christian thing, sir."

"Jesus Christ, boy. It's your time then. I ain't wasting mine putting a passel of Papist greasers 'neath the ground. Not when we're this close I ain't. You do what you want."

Penmark raked him with a contemptuous stare, then turned and walked to his horse. Getting the canteen from his saddle, he carried it to the rock-edged well and cranked up a bucket of water to fill it. Jason stared at him a bitter moment, then got his own canteen and followed suit. . . .

They had come a goodly way in forty-eight hours, counting two breaks for sleep, and of course they hadn't dared press the horses too hard. Even so, Jason was tired to the marrow, drained by the searing heat. Hardened by years of tramping behind a plow and more recently by working cattle, he was hard put to match the tireless drive of this man nearly forty years his elder. Penmark had more than an iron constitution. He was a man totally obsessed. Jason had a strong reason of his own, but even the stamina of a tough eighteen-year-old had its limits.

Tall and big-boned himself, Jason Drum hadn't yet filled out with a solid maturity to match his size. His sweat-patched shirt hung like a rag on his cord-muscled trunk; his arms and legs gangled awkwardly. Though he usually carried himself with a neat wiry grace that made up for his awkwardness, he was drag footed with exhaustion now, queasy and shaken by what he'd just witnessed; his step was stiff and plodding. The tan of his thin face, a face that seemed too sober for its years, had yielded to a ruddy burn below the brim of his old slouch hat. His sandy hair was sun streaked, his big-knuckled hands stiffly swollen, and they shook enough to spill water as he filled his canteen.

The two men drank their fill, watered their animals at the trough, then mounted and rode away on a trail that now bent somewhat southeasterly out of Corazon. Neither looked back at the smoking carnage of the station. The Santa Rita mountains rose in dim purple serrations to the south; more dimly yet, ranging south and west into Mexico, rolled the San Ignacios. Except for a

11

slight change of shape, the peaks seemed no nearer than they'd been a day ago.

Jason and Penmark had been part of a posse that had ridden out of New Hope two days ago, but the others of their party had given up the chase in less than a day. You couldn't blame them. High June had turned the land to a baking desolation; even those possemen who weren't storekeepers or other counter-jumpers of the same ilk had little taste for tackling it. The posse had been ill prepared to start with, while the seven men who'd robbed the New Hope Bank had laid the groundwork for their escape only too well. Having extra saddle mounts and packhorses, they could hold well ahead of any pursuit with no danger of riding their animals into the ground.

At first it had been almost touch and go. The hastily organized posse had ridden out of town minutes behind the escaping robbers. The latter hadn't gone far before they'd split into two pairs and one trio, afterward forking off on three widely separated routes—another move that appeared to have been nicely calculated in advance. Since they'd had no time to divide the loot, they obviously intended to rendezvous somewhere to the south. Maybe in Mexico. Coming to where the trail had broken three ways, the posse had separated too, splitting up four men to a group. Jason and Penmark had joined two others on the main trail, that of the bandit trio.

Their companions—Manly Jones, who owned the livery stable, and a rancher named Trautmann—had

12

given up yesterday morning and turned back toward New Hope. They'd had good reasons for abandoning the chase. Both were family men; neither had a compelling motive for continuing a pursuit where all advantage lay with the pursued. As Trautmann, the stolid Teuton, had pointed out, their own supply of water and provisions, thrown quickly together in the need for haste, wasn't sufficient to stretch much further. With their horses tiring beneath them, they were losing ground by the hour. Damned risky to proceed farther into a barren country none of them knew well enough to be sure of finding water. Something the robbers had surely packed in abundance. *Ja,* and besides, there was Cayetano. . . .

The Chiricahua war chief was up from his stronghold in the Sierra Madres again, cutting a zigzag of lightning raids across a wide swath of southern Arizona. Cayetano made a deadly game of it, hitting where the army and the loosely scattered civil population least expected. Both Miles and Crook had failed to run him down in other years, and the wily Apache had never pressed his guerilla activities too heavily. Making casual strikes into both American and Mexican territory where and when it suited him, he could always fall back to his mountain retreat. A periodic nuisance, he was rarely a severe one. Yet he had an uncanny talent for organizing the chronic malcontents of the Apache tribes; he was a flawless tactician and even a strategist of sorts. Lazily exercising what seemed to be a purely racial vendetta, never taking his own game too seriously, he was a capricious and unpredictable enemy. Just now he had the whole territory jittery as hell.

The towns were safe, but travel between them had died to a trickle. East-west stage runs had ceased a couple weeks back. Men making journeys of any length traveled in groups, armed to the teeth. Mine operators hired gangs of tough nuts to guard their ore wagons from mines to milling plants. Troops of cavalry had been dispatched from New Mexico to strengthen the garrisons at Forts Bowie and Stambaugh. Nervous ranchers didn't range far from their headquarters and slept with rifles by their beds. Since Apaches doted on slim odds, a posse of twelve heavily armed men might tackle a trek across hostile territory with some confidence, provided the trail didn't stretch too far. But broken into fours, each party was a sitting duck. Sure, Cayetano might be a hundred miles away. But there was no telling. The fear of never knowing was fed by the furnace-like heat that pressed on a man's senses like a deadening hand; by the deadly oppressiveness of this scarred and sun-blasted land, whose mesas and *playas* were threaded by a few lonely roads that linked its ranches, mining hamlets, and roadhouses. No, you couldn't blame Jones and Trautmann for turning back. . . .

Jason Drum wasn't reckless or foolish. Working with his muscles on a daylight-to-dark grind since he was ten had burned all the ordinary restless bravura of youth out of his system. He didn't smile much; there was little in his young life to smile about. He had his

14

share of Missouri mulishness, but it wasn't unthinking stubbornness, either, that kept him at the relentless Penmark's side long after good sense had told him that the whole business had turned into a long-odds gamble just about any way you looked at it.

Old Man Penmark simply didn't give a damn. Nothing, not even his own life, mattered next to accomplishing what he'd set out to do. He'd accomplish it or die in the attempt. You couldn't help wondering if Penmark was looking for death. The thought gave Jason a ripple of gooseflesh. But the older man's granite mask was never cracked by even a self-revealing twitch. . . . You couldn't be sure.

Jason's own driving desperation to overhaul the robbers might not have carried him this far if it hadn't been for coming on a place yesterday, around high noon, where the three men had rested before going on. Strips of blood-crusted cloth they'd discarded had told the story. One man had been wounded in the shooting fracas with townsmen before the escape. Still losing blood, he must be in serious condition by now. A fact, Penmark had grimly observed, that was bound to start slowing them.

Penmark, reading the sign, had announced at nightfall that they'd begun overtaking the trio of fugitives. By mid-morning today it was apparent that the trail was bending southwest toward Corazon. Whatever the wounded man's companions had meant to do at the swing station, get care for him or perhaps just leave him there, they hadn't lingered. Nothing that was left

15

in the wake of an Apache raid would be of any use to a seriously injured, perhaps dying man. So the three had pushed on, quartering back toward their original route and an unknown rendezvous. . . .

The trail was straightening into a southward line again. Penmark rode slowly in the lead, holding the track with a hard-bitten patience. He followed it easily and intently, sometimes bending from his saddle to study it out better. Jason rode loose and slumped; the burn of raw sunlight darkened his eyes. He thought of the cool cottonwoods at the home place. His mother and sisters would be relaxing under them right now, taking a break in the day's work and sipping lemonade or buttermilk.

"Mr. Penmark," he said.

"Yeah."

"What happens when we come up on 'em?"

Penmark didn't take his eyes off the ground. "Got another bug in your belly, Drum?"

"No sir, I just wondered—"

"I tell you what don't happen. These men are killers. What we don't do, we take no damnfool chances with 'em."

"I just wondered how we will do it."

"It'll go how it goes." Penmark swung his head up, locking stares. "You want to back out, say so now."

"I ain't backing out."

"These men got nothing to lose, boy. When the shooting starts, it's them or us. You ever hit anything with that squirrel iron of yours?"

"Sir, I make myself a middling good shot."

Penmark's lips pursed up in a wait-and-see twist. "Man ain't a squirrel. I don't look for a whole hell of a lot from you, Drum. Just don't get in my way."

He bent back to his tracking. Jason rode in a resentful silence, rolling spit with his tongue. He was scared right enough, but no call for Penmark to set him down. He was here, wasn't he?

Yet he had to ask how logical his reason was now. Penmark figured the gang had split up without dividing the loot; these three they were trailing might not be packing a cent of it. Could turn out a pretty fruitless chase from his standpoint. But he'd had to take that chance; he couldn't just do nothing. Wondering if the possemen who'd followed the other bandits had given up as Jones and Trautmann had, he decided it was likely. None but he and Penmark had deep reasons. . . .

They were pressing into rougher country. Sand-colored cliffs and spurs broke up the flats; the two men struck gravelly stretches where nothing grew but bear grass and prickly pear. White sparks of light danced off the mica-laced ground. Penmark was frequently dismounting now to look for sign. Checked to a slower pace, he was getting restless and angry, muttering to himself.

"You sure we're heading right, Mr. Penmark?"

"Use your goddam eyes," Penmark said savagely. "I am tracking most by blood drops you can see yourself. That hurt one is throwing blood. He's in a bad way.

They got to stop soon. Goddamit, they got to!"

The sun slanted lower, painting the rocky scape with a pink-orange glare. Sunset wasn't far off. The dead quilt of heat lifted a little, and it was comparatively cool in the lee of cliffs where the long shadows grew. Passing through a lacy green fog of mesquite, they came to the edge of a shallow valley. Penmark raised his hand for a halt and pulled back off the skyline, studying the scene below. The slopes were littered with splintered blocks of sandstone and cut by several deep notches. The long and narrow valley floor was partly masked by thickets of mesquite and catclaw and some scrubby oaks.

There was a lot of cover down there, Jason thought, but he couldn't see anything out of the ordinary. You'd make them out if they were on the move, horseback. If they had stopped, it would be harder. No trace of smoke. But even figuring they'd shed pursuit, they might not risk a fire in country where the Apaches were out.

"They're down there," Penmark said abruptly.

"I don't see nothing."

That green-slate stare. Penmark spat. "Boy, I wouldn't expect you to kick up a frozen turd in a mule-yard on a cold morning. They're down there. I'm going to take them. You hark close and do what I tell you."

II

Penmark laid out the plan in a precise, intent, steel-hard voice, as if he were daring Jason to misunderstand a word. It was simple enough. Jason would merely bait the trap; he, Penmark, would close it. He pointed out where the men were encamped, a dense clot of brush near the valley's center. Studying it through the field glasses Penmark passed him, Jason managed to pick out one of the robbers' tethered horses through the screening brush: a dun animal that was almost the color of the ground. Penmark had spotted it without the glasses; he'd also noted movement in the brush thereabouts. He figured they could get onto the valley floor without being seen by slipping down through one of the wedge-shaped notches in the slope, and Jason was to try for Christ's sake not to make too much noise.

"All you got to worry about is your end of it," Penmark told him with the same controlled, stony care, as though addressing an idiot. "You got hardly anything to do. Just stay down. They can't see you and you can't get hit. Any of 'em comes poking your way, you got all the advantage. You're on the ground and you can hear him and see him first."

Leaving their horses ground-hitched back in the mesquite, the two quarter-skirted around the valley's rim to its east flank. For the descent, Penmark chose the second deep cleft they came to. It was a brush-

19

filled ravine that scored deep into the earth and rock, following the down-slope clear to its bottom. Jason tried not to make noise as he followed Penmark, but the brush ripped at his clothes; every snapped twig sounded like a gunshot. It was hard going down the steep jumble of broken rock, which kept turning under his boots; his rifle and the coiled rope he carried over one shoulder didn't help his balance. Luckily the rubble was too large to make much sound as it grated and stirred beneath his driving feet.

Stealth was hard to manage when you were big built, over six feet tall, and made clumsy by pure exhaustion. Jason couldn't remember feeling so bone tired in his life, and he wondered if it was partly fear. But his mind was razor tense. It must all be the deadly heat and the long hours in saddle. Nor had they gotten much sleep on the night stops. Val Penmark would keep pushing right up till dark and have them rolling out in the gray light before dawn, soon as track showed.

Penmark was iron. Pure iron. He moved with a stiff grace and contained his exhaustion as he did his rage—as if it were a trained tiger.

Once they were on the bottom, it was easier to move quietly. The masses of brush grew enough apart for the two men to slide between them, their bodies balled in awkward crouches, as most of the foliage wasn't chest-high to a man. Jason, totally unsure of the camp's position now, blindly followed Penmark's lead.

Suddenly the older man motioned for a halt and raised his head, listening intently. Straining his ears,

Jason picked out the faint mutter of men's voices.

They moved on, Penmark picking the way with slow care. Sweat glided down Jason's ribs, made a stinging wash in his eyes; he sleeved it away without pausing. When the voices seemed uncomfortably loud, Penmark stopped again and studied the terrain around them. He pointed wordlessly at a cluster of scrub oak that reared taller than the green clouds of mesquite around it. Jason nodded, slipping the coiled rope off his shoulder as Penmark glided away to his right, the brush swallowing him.

Working quickly, Jason fastened the rope's end around one stem of the oak clump, then moved away through the mesquite thickets, paying out line. When the lariat was gently taut, its full length uncoiled, he stretched out on his belly beneath a screen of mesquite and gave the rope a sharp tug that rattled the oak leaves. Twice more he jerked it before a break in the drift of voices told him they'd caught the sound.

A long trailing silence. Again Jason yanked the rope.

He heard one man speak quietly, as if giving an order. Jason lay motionless then, his heart thudding against the earth. Brush crackled; slow steps crunched the flinty soil. Penmark had hoped the trick might pull the wounded robber's companions into the open, but they were being cagey. Only one of them was coming this way. Jason heard the sharp click of a pistol being cocked; the man was close, but there was no sign of him. Must be prowling through the brush in a deep crouch so he wouldn't expose his head and shoulders.

The steps paused. Jason jerked the line once more.

Suddenly the stalker fired into the oak thicket three times. Leaves and twigs showered down, and Jason promptly hauled the rope taut. Part of the oak scrub sprang sideways as if a man concealed there had limply toppled and bent it. That was what the rifleman was supposed to think. But would he? Would it draw him into the open? . . . .

Jason could hear him moving again. Following the sound with his eyes, Jason saw the man's blocky head and shoulders lift to view, and then he was tramping warily out of the brush—a chunky fellow whose Sonora hat cut a hard slant of shadow across his swarthy face. Coming straight on toward the oak thicket, he'd discover the ruse in another moment.

Jason tightly fisted his rifle. Would he have to shoot? Buck fever grabbed him; he began to shake. Where was Penmark? He was supposed to . . .

A rifle's clear, splitting report came. The chunky man spun like a top and went down.

"Miguel!" his companion yelled.

Getting no answer, he came plowing through the brush on the run. The crash of sound broke Jason's paralysis. Coming up on his knees, he levered his Winchester and, as the second man came bursting into the open, shot quickly.

He made a clean miss.

Not pausing in his run, the tall robber veered sideways, loping in a bent-over run into more brush that abruptly cut off Jason's view.

22

Jason fired blindly at the sound. The man was cutting around him in a wide arc, seeking a better vantage point. And then Penmark's rifle spoke again. The robber pulled to a halt—or was he hit?

Another hot drowsing silence. If he wasn't hit, Jason thought, at least he realized he was facing two rifles, not one. Through a break in the brush, Jason could see the chunky Mexican sprawled on his face fifty feet away. He had made no movement.

Jason strained his ears for the hint of a sound. Finally he raised his voice in a shout, "Mr. Penmark!"

No reply.

Jason crawled to his feet and moved forward in a slow crouch, threading between the thickets. Penmark was either unsure he'd hit the tall man or else knew he hadn't. Either way, Jason reasoned, Penmark was likely to be working silently nearer the man's position. Might be they could catch him between them. . . .

A shot clipped through the mesquite two feet from Jason. He dived to the ground, slamming heavily on his chest, hugging the gravel in a burst of gritty sweat. No other shot came. The robber must have fired at some tell-tale sound. Cautiously Jason pushed himself up on his hands, peering through the tangle of mesquite and broken rock ahead of him.

Then he caught a flicker of motion. In the same moment Penmark's rifle opened up again. The tall man was falling back the way he'd come. Toward the camp. And the horses. Jason tried to bring his rifle to bear, but intervening brush gave him only fleeting glimpses of

23

the running man. Then he was cut off.

On the heels of the tall robber's retreat, Jason heard another scramble of sound off to his left. The Mexican! Apparently not hard hit, he'd been playing possum; he too was making for the horses.

Too late to cut him off. Jason headed after him in a heedless run; Penmark was breaking brush in the same direction. Momentarily all four of them were converging on the brush-hidden camp from different angles.

But the two robbers reached it first. Suddenly both were shooting from its concealment, using rifles now. Jason hit the ground again; he had a glimpse of Penmark, only yards away now, lunging for the shelter of a sandstone spur. Gunfire hammered against Jason's ears, as Penmark, partly exposing himself, returned the robbers' fire, pumping shots into the brush as fast as he could.

Sudden hoofbeats then, followed by a crash of thickets. The two were making a break from the other side of the packed brush. From here it cut them off completely. Cursing, Penmark sprang up and skirted the heaviest brush at a run, Jason following.

The valley was scantily brushed toward its south end; the two men, flattened to their horses' necks, were streaking across it at an all-out run. Penmark braced to a halt, raised his rifle, and sighted carefully. His shot sent the tall man's horse crashing to the ground. Twisting free of his falling animal, the robber landed heavily, rolling over and over.

He staggered to his feet almost at once. Penmark drew bead again; his firing pin fell on an empty chamber. He dropped the gun and wheeled on Jason, his face livid.

"Your rifle, boy!"

Jason didn't have time to relinquish his grip on the Winchester; it was wrenched from his hands. The Mexican twisted in his saddle, then yanked his fiddle-footing black to a stop. He whipped around and headed back for his companion. The tall man put his head down and ran, straining for speed. Penmark began to fire with a steady, dogged fury, swearing as he tried to sight in the unfamiliar weapon. Shots kicked up powdery fans near the running man's legs.

Suddenly he went down, somersaulting in his run, staggered up again, and almost fell on his first step. He was hit, his right leg dragging. The Mexican careened his animal up beside him and tried to help him swing up behind. But the Mexican's own wounded arm was flapping and useless. Reaching out his good arm, he lost control of his horse. It shuffled away from the tall man's effort to mount; he couldn't brace his bad leg, and it gave way when he tried to swing up the other leg.

One of Penmark's bullets must have seared the black. It lunged into a panicky run, as the tall man, limping alongside, made another wild grab for the Mexican's arm. He stumbled, his hold slipped, and he plunged down in a moil of dust.

Unable to control his horse, the Mexican lost his

nerve. He sank his spurs with a hoarse yell, and then the black was racing away toward the valley's end. The tall man rolled dazedly to a sitting position and watched them go.

Penmark was already running stiffly forward, rifle half-pointed, and Jason was on his heels. They were yards away from the downed man as the Mexican drove his mount recklessly up a broad notch in the far slope. Moments later the escaping robber had topped the rim and was gone.

Penmark's face was wolfish, the lips peeled back from his teeth, as he tramped up to the man on the ground and halted. His lifted rifle was pointed at the robber's head. Jason thought for a moment of wild disbelief that Penmark meant to kill him.

The man raised his sweaty face; it was square and heavy-boned, divided by deep looping mustaches. His hat lay yards away; his curly black hair was matted to his head. He was brown as an Indian, but his eyes were steely blue. He reached a hand to his hip.

"You touch that hogleg," Penmark said tonelessly, "and I'll blow your head off."

The man's broad mouth grinned. A couple tiny scars grooved one corner of it, touching the grin with a wry irony. "From your look, sir, you wouldn't need that much reason."

"I got just one reason for keeping you alive. There's a few things I want to know."

"Can't oblige you if I bleed to death first." He motioned at his dusty pantsleg where a spreading stain

26

of red showed above the boot. "I was reaching for something to tie it off with . . ."

"Boy, you get his gun. Go careful."

Jason bent, pulled a .44 Colt from the holster at the tall man's side, and stepped back. The robber took a greasy bandanna from his pocket and knotted it around his leg below the knee.

"That'll do you now. Stand up. What's your name?"

The man grimaced as he heaved stiffly to his feet, holding his weight on his good leg. Big-shouldered and whittle-hipped, he stood an inch or so taller than either Penmark or Jason. He had a hard and dangerous look coupled with a curious dignity and a mannered speech. It made Jason wonder what kind of a cross-dog specimen they'd snared.

"John Heath, gentlemen, at your service."

"Captain Jack Heath?"

"If you like."

Neither name meant anything to Jason. But Penmark gave a slow nod as if it explained everything. "There ain't a judge in the territory would summon me to docket if I blowed you apart where you stand."

"I fancy not."

"You goddam right not. So mister, you do's you're told and don't bat a winker wrong. Or you won't even live to see a hangrope."

Heath's smile flickered and went. "You present a most engaging choice." He glanced at his dead horse. "You killed a fine animal there, my friend. I set a good deal of store by him."

"You're luckier'n some." Penmark moved his rifle barrel in a short arc. "To your camp. Your other man, the hurt one, he there?"

"Dead. He died less than an hour ago."

"You're still lucky," Penmark said softly. "Get walking."

"Young man, if you'll hand me my hat . . ."

Jason got the black, flat-crowned *ranchero* hat and took it to him. With Heath limping slowly ahead, they moved back to the mottle of scrub oak that hid the camp. The sun had dropped to a flat molten stain on the west rim, shedding a reddish light that barely reached to the gloomy hollow inside the tight-growing scrub. Five horses were tied there; some gear was piled in an orderly fashion to one side. A covered body lay on the ground. There was a half-dug grave, a couple of Bowie knives stuck in the pile of loose earth beside it. Penmark lifted the blanket from the dead man's face, grunted, and lowered it.

"You surprised us in the act of laying a comrade to rest," Heath murmured. "Don't suppose one of you might consent to finish the job."

"Buzzards can have the bastard for all of me," Penmark said. "Drum there, he likes dead folks buried. Ask him."

Heath smiled twistedly. He eased down on his rump, gripping his bloody leg over the wound. "Well, Mr. Drum, you'll only need one of the knives for that. Mind handing me the other? Like to fix that leg a bit. If your friend doesn't object."

Penmark tramped to the mound of fresh dirt and swept his boot sideward, kicking one of the Bowies over by Heath. "You make small moves with that sticker and no sudden ones. Or you be planted in the same hole. Drum, fetch the horses down here. Look for some grass while you're about it. Good a place as any to spend the night."

His muscles leaden with exhaustion, Jason slogged back toward the notch. Scanning about, he spotted a scant lacing of bear grass hard by the east slope. After leading their horses down from the rim, he hobbled them on the grass, then packed his and Penmark's plunder to the camp, got the robbers' horses and did the same for them. He wished he could water the animals, but the bottom of this valley was dry as a bone. His and Penmark's horses had watered at Corazon and so, he supposed, had the robbers' saddle mounts and packhorses. It would have to do them for a time.

Dusk was starting to gray the reddish light as he tramped back to camp, so tired he could hardly lift one foot after the other. Penmark was squatting on his heels, rifle across his knees, eyes half-lidded like a lizard's as he watched Heath finish the job of bandaging his leg. He'd slit his pantsleg to the knee and washed his knot-muscled calf, which the bullet had gone clean through. The wound was a pulpy mess in a dark welter of bruised flesh. Heath ripped up a spare shirt to plug the wound and tie around it.

"Well, you did miss the bone, friend." His jaw muscles rippled with the twisted grin. "Is that what you mean by 'luck'?"

Penmark said flatly, "Fetch wood, boy. Fix some grub."

"Mr. Penmark, I want to know if he's got the money."

"We'll see to that directly. It's drawing dark fast. Get us a fire built."

Jason, on the edge of telling him to go to hell, bit back the words and dragged himself to the task. There was plenty of dead brush close around; in a few minutes he had a sizeable armload. He staggered back to the glade and dropped it, then dug out matches and began to lay a fire.

Heath settled his back against an oak trunk, his leg straight out before him, and pulled a slim black cheroot from his pocket. "Throw me a match, will you, son? Don't know if it's occurred to you, old pot," to Penmark, "but a fire makes smoke."

"It's drawing dark. Anyways, Drum's an ole country boy. Knows how to make a fire that's 'most smokeless. You *can* do that, can't you, boy?"

Jason nodded, gritting his teeth. He flipped a match over to Heath. The tall man caught it, snapped it into flame on his thumbnail, and fired up his cheroot. His eyes glinted through the smoke. "Apaches, of course, might pick up woodsmoke ten miles off if the wind's right. Freakish thing, a wind current."

Penmark moved his head in negation. "We don't camp with no fire and you to watch. There'll be one or other of us watching you all night long, sonny boy, and he'll have plenty light to shoot by."

Heath chuckled out smoke. "You know, I never thought of that." He gazed at the slow soaking of his bandage as fresh blood dyed it. "Nasty hole, that. Really ought to rest the leg a day or so. And you chaps look as though you might stand a bit of rest yourselves."

"Might be handy for you if I figured so. That greaser who got away, he might just fetch back some help back here."

"Ah yes. Then I'd have a reason for stalling you or at least slowing you, wouldn't I?"

"We followed seven of you out of New Hope. One's dead. You're taken. Say none of the rest are, they will show up at your rendezvous. If the Mex makes it, he can lead 'em back to us. 'Pending how far from here you meant to meet up."

"You're almighty sure we did."

"To split up ten thousand in paper greenbacks. I call that a good reason. Soon's you get that fire going, you can look through his plunder, boy."

"You might save yourself the trouble," Heath said agreeably. "I don't have a plugged cent of the loot."

All the same, Jason felt a feverish glow of hope as he began to rifle through the camp gear. Turning up even a good part of the stolen money would serve his end of things. But a few minutes' search of the bandits' possessions rocked him back into a heavy-footed gloom.

"There ain't nothing in his possibles, Mr. Penmark.

Just a few coins. Mexican from the look."

Penmark grunted. "I still lay odds he knows where the loot is. He's the big mucky-muck of that bunch. They didn't have time to split the money, or where's his share? They trust anyone with all of it, I figure it be him. Lay odds he left all of it cached back some'eres along the trail."

Heath grinned. "Now why would I do that?"

"You and the Mex was slowed considerable by the wounded one. You had no idea how many men might be on your trail. Could be two, could be twenty. But even fearful of being overtaken, you wouldn't drop your hurt man. Even a bastard like you's got a code about that. So it'd be insurance, kind of, to hide the money some'eres along the way. Say you and the Mex got caught up with and taken. Say your boys heard about it and also that the loot hadn't been recovered. They would be damn eager to bust you free, seeing you'd know where the money was hid. Even supposing you didn't get caught, be easy enough to pick up the loot later."

"A shrewd guess, old pot. But a guess."

"Hell, I couldn't care less." Penmark glanced indifferently at Jason. "Too bad for you, Drum. 'Less you can make him tell where it is, you are shit out of luck."

Heath showed his strong teeth amusedly. "And of course *you're* not interested?"

Penmark spat. "Mister, I couldn't give less a goddam. I had no money in that matchbox of a bank. Never trusted 'em. You want to make this cocky son of a bitch talk, Drum?"

32

Jason stared at him a moment, blinking in a fog of angry exhaustion, closing and unclosing his fists. Then he sat down by the fire and looked into it. Penmark made a contemptuous sound with his teeth and tongue. "He's a good Christian boy, Drum is. You had something I want, I'd tear your goddam heart out by the roots if need be."

"I fancy you would." Heath eyed him curiously. "Just what the Sheol *do* you want? I know there was a good-sized posse on our heels at the start. Even assuming you split to take up our separate trails, there must have been more than just the two of you tracking Miguel and Artie and me. . . ."

"Others quit. We had cause not to."

"Huh. And your piece of the pie, young fellow . . . money?"

"My family's whole savings was in that bank," Jason said dully. "All we been able to lay aside in years."

"Huh," Heath said again. "But you, sir, never used a bank."

Penmark was sitting cross-legged. He leaned slightly forward, firelight washing wickedly against his eyes. "My wife did. Had herself an account in that New Hope matchbox. Was in there on business when you and your high-graders held it up."

Heath's eyes narrowed. "Yes?"

"There was shooting. She got a bullet."

"Dead?"

"Straight off. With a bullet in the head."

"There was a spot of shooting," Heath said slowly.

33

"One fool in the bank went for a gun."

"My wife didn't do nothing. She didn't do a goddam thing. All she done was go to the bank to put in some money."

"It must have been a stray shot. Might have been as easily fired by one of the New Hope men as by us." Heath shrugged. "I didn't know. It was a bloody confusion after the shooting began. We had to fight our way out. . . ."

"I tell you what." Canted forward in his intensity, Penmark drove the butt of his rifle hard against the ground. The raised scar of a cut, which had once laid bare the bone, gleamed white across his knuckles. "You shut your goddam mouth about it and maybe you will reach New Hope alive."

"For the hangman." Heath smiled, trickling out a stream of smoke. "So, you know I'm already wanted for a killing or two. It gives you something to think about, eh?"

"No. For you to think about. Every mile of the goddam way. That's why I don't gutshoot you now, you slimy bastard."

III

Jason threw together a meal of sorts but hadn't much appetite for his share of it. Penmark told him to take the first sleep since he was too drag-assed to trust on guard. They'd split the night into four two-hour shifts, two apiece. He rolled into his soogans and fell into a dreamless sleep that wasn't broken till Penmark shook him awake. Jason took up the guard duty feeling considerably freshened. The cool of night was pleasant; it was easeful just to sit and do nothing but keep the fire up. Heath wouldn't bear much watching, for Penmark had tied his hands back of him and lashed them to an oak trunk. A great horned owl belled somewhere in the night. Otherwise, except for Penmark's snoring, it was pretty quiet.

Feeling depressed about the money and all, Jason felt the sight of the covered body start to nag him. Even an outlaw had a right to be laid under like a white man. He knew Penmark would refuse to let him take the time for it come morning. Going about it quiet as he could, Jason got one of the Bowies and began hacking earth out of the unfinished grave. It was tough loosening the stony soil, and after half an hour he'd sunk the hole only a couple feet more. Common sense warned him not to exhaust himself again. He rolled the blanket tight around the dead man and quickly filled the shallow grave, packing the rocks and flinty earth tight to seal it against scavengers.

"Good boy."

Heath spoke softly as he finished smoothing off the mound. Jason jerked around, seeing the outlaw curled awkwardly on his side as he'd been, but his eyes open. Picking up his rifle, Jason sat down cross-legged and watched the man. You could almost see the thoughts crawling behind Heath's eyes. Not what he was thinking, of course. But you could guess. Grunting,

Heath tried to ease his position.

"A fellow can't catch much sleep this way. Look, son, you've got the rifle and I've a wounded leg. You wouldn't imperil my captivity by cutting me free of this damned tree. You can leave my hands tied."

"Mr. Penmark wants you like you are. I guess you better stay that way."

Heath's lips quirked upward. "You know, Drum, you're in a worse bind than I am. Letting that crusty old turd run you about like a squaw."

"He don't run me."

"No? From what I've seen, all he'd need do is holler cricket and you'd chirp."

Jason's face began to bum, but he knew what Heath was trying to do. "What I think is you being tied to a tree is sense, no matter who ordered it."

"But his order all the same, eh?" Heath yawned. "Where do you hail from, ole country boy?"

"Outside of New Hope?"

"I mean to start with. Missouri? I thought so. And your people—tater 'n turnip mud farmers, I'd wager."

Jason picked up a short branch and began whittling at it with short angry whacks. "My pap pulled stakes for Arizona three years ago. There was him and Ma and five of us kids. It took all we had to buy up a little cow outfit and make a new start. Didn't hardly clear enough for two years to pay a couple hands while Pa and me learned about beef cows. Typhus took Pa last year. Him and my two little brothers. There's me, Ma, my two sisters left."

"Three women to see after, eh? A tough row for you."

"Not as bad's it might of been. We held on, all of us pitching in and our two hands sticking by. Didn't look to clear no big profit this year but had a piece of luck. Indian agent from the San Lazaro reservation come down looking for cattle to fill out his beef allotment. A rancher up north was supposed to supply him, but couldn't meet his contract. So lots of us small-loop outfits around New Hope was tapped to make up the difference. Got paid in good government cash for our beef. But I guess you know that."

"Oh yes. We heard." A chuckle rippled Heath's jaw. "As your friend said, that New Hope bank's a matchbox. We knew that too. It wasn't outfitted to handle large windfalls of cash from its depositors. No guard, an old-fashioned safe. No town marshal. The county seat fifty miles away and no sheriff's deputy, even, assigned to New Hope. Town almost empty on a mid-week day, hardly anyone about but old codgers dozing on porches. We expected the job to be a plum. Nothing like the spirited resistance we ran into."

"Happened me and a few other people from ranches was in town. Like Mr. Penmark and his wife."

Heath shrugged. "A rum go about the woman, but it's done. Why all the talk suddenly, boy? Trying to arouse my sympathy for your loss?"

"I don't look for much of that from you, mister."

"Wise lad."

"But say you know where the money is, it's no use to

you now. You couldn't lose nothing by telling."

"Wrong. I can look for help from my men only if I deal them square. Say I hid the loot as Penmark thinks. Miguel knows where it is too. He'll tell the others. They're my best hope of getting out of this with a whole hide . . . help that won't be forthcoming if I betray where I hid the money."

Jason's teeth tightened together till his jaws ached. "You might be lucky to live that long. Mr. Penmark's on a hairtrigger about you as is. He gets it in his head to do for you, you needn't look to me for help."

"There's head money on me, Drum. . . ."

"I don't know nothing about that."

"I fancy Penmark does. Ask him. All you need do is fetch me to the law intact. A railroad company, several banks, the Territory of Arizona have offered various rewards for my capture. Assuming my men won't overhaul you before we reach New Hope, you stand to collect all of several thousand dollars . . . just for keeping me alive."

An instant suspicion mingled with Jason's flare of hope. "I'd say," he said thinly, "you are trying to set me and Mr. Penmark at odds with each other."

Heath showed the edge of a smile. "I might be, at that. But it's most likely I merely concur with your opinion."

"What?"

"That my chances may stretch rather fine without your help. I'm afraid, Drum, that your companion is a little mad."

· · ·

The sun was well up as they started north next morning. Val Penmark seemed tired, old beyond his years, his voice a dragging grunt as he gave the order to break camp. In spite of the danger that Heath's men might pose, they rode at a plodding gait, drained by three days of pressing a savage pace on the high-summer desert. Now that Penmark had the gang's kingpin in hand, his driving fury seemed to have shriveled away. He rode in a stiff slump and never looked back. Heath followed behind him, hands tied in front so he could manage his reins. The outlaw was showing the effects of his injury and a near-sleepless night. His face was puffy red with a touch of fever, but he rode with his head up.

Leading the string of pack animals, Jason held the rear, nervously alert. He kept twisting glances back and around. But in all that dun-colored waste he saw nothing that he hadn't been seeing for going on four days, and his alertness began to blur away with the sheer monotony of it. Flats of gray sage, scatterings of scrub oak and manzanita, smoke trees shrouding the zigzag arroyos, all merged into one scene of neutral desolation. Poppies and paintbrush, the red stipples of ocotillo in bloom made the only dashes of color; lemon light hit the redrock ridges with a raw glare. What's the difference, he thought dully. Apaches or white outlaws, it would be all the same if they were attacked—he wouldn't pick up the signs of danger in time.

Not his kind of country. He thought of Pa, that tough

39

luckless man who had broken his back and his heart trying to crop the stony, worn-out Missouri acres that his father and grandfather had tilled before him. The Drums had always been hardscrabble; they seemed born to be. All the dedication and hard work of four generations hadn't improved their line by a lick, and before that their folks had been tenant people in the north of England. So pulling stakes never helped either. New Hope. Another name for old discouragement. Still, a man had to keep trying. What else was there?

A mother and two young sisters. Which was a good deal, come down to it. Drums had a deep family way. They'd be mortally afraid for him, a worry to eat deeper each passing day. They'd have sent to town for word of him and would know what he was about and why. Returning empty-handed . . . after all this. It grated like bitter sand in his craw.

Still there was Heath. Penmark had surlily allowed, when Jason had asked, that there might be a price of sorts on the outlaw's head. A dim ray in the pan maybe, but it was something.

Penmark called a stop at noon. They rested on the bottom of a broad wash where the smoke trees threw a silky-hot shade. Jason untied Heath so he could look to his leg. The calf was so swollen that Heath had to rip his boot-top with a knife to pull the boot free of his foot. He tore the caked mess of a bandage slowly away, pain making the flesh groove white around his mouth. The wound was draining clean, about all you could say for it. He looked up, a sheen of sweat on his face.

"I say, Drum. There's a bottle of whiskey in that small pack. Would you break it out?"

Jason rose off his haunches, but Penmark was nearest the horses; he plodded over, undid the diamond hitch, and dumped the pack to the ground. Getting the bottle out, he straightened up. Opening his hand without a word, he let the bottle fall. It shattered to pieces on a rock.

Jason eased warily to his feet, watching Penmark's eyes. "Sir," he said carefully, "there was no cause to do that."

Penmark kept staring fixedly at Heath. "I'll say what's to be, pup. You keep your goddam lip cinched."

"Man," Heath said softly, "the heat's frying your brains. Listen. I didn't kill your wife. Whoever did that shot wild. I don't shoot wild."

"Did or didn't, it's on your head. You head up that scum. You planned it start to finish."

"What's the difference now, old man? It won't bring her back."

"Shut your rotten mouth," Penmark said in a reedy whisper.

Heath's squinted gaze flicked to Jason. "You've a small interest in my staying alive, Drum. Why don't you fetch me some water?"

Jason sidled stiffly toward the canteen he had laid in a rock shadow. Penmark tipped up his rifle. "He don't need water. There's little enough to see us through."

A hot anger boiled up in Jason. "Him too, Mr. Penmark. I had enough of you saying what's to be."

"I'm saying it again, boy. You had your own drink. Leave that water be."

Jason set his jaw and moved on toward the canteen. Penmark's turning stare followed him; so did the rifle muzzle. Halting by the canteen, Jason hesitated. Penmark's eyes were frozen beyond expression. God, would he? Don't think about it, do it. He's got to be stood up to.

Jason bent, reaching for the canteen.

In that moment, with Jason and Penmark fixed on each other, Heath made his try. One moment he was slumped almost prone; the next he was rolling sideways in a long-muscled burst of energy, grabbing for Jason's rifle where the youth had leaned it against a rock several yards away. The move caught Jason flat-footed. But Penmark reacted with a smooth, contemptuous ease, taking three long steps toward Heath.

In those same fleeting seconds, Heath seized the rifle, levered it, and scrambled to his knees. As he swung it up, Penmark's leg lashed out in a powerful kick. His boot smashed against Heath's cheekbone with a force that flung him on his back. Penmark bent and scooped up the rifle and tossed it to Jason, all in one movement.

"You ain't fitten for orders 'cept taking 'em," Penmark said meagerly. "You want to argufy it, now's the time."

Shaken, Jason could only stare at the gun in his hands, then at Penmark. Heath groaned and struggled

42

to a sitting position. A strawberry stain of mashed skin discolored the side of his face.

"You could of shot," Jason began. And let the words die there.

Penmark's taut face seemed to change as he watched it, loosening into tired lines and wattles. His slitted gaze probed at Jason as if he didn't know him. Slowly, slowly, he let the rifle slack downward.

"Too quick." His voice was gray and dull, an old man's voice. "I don't want it quick with him. Tie his hands. Then give him water. One cup, no more."

Nobody said a word through the long afternoon. The sun broiled against their backs and left sides, and finally heeled down toward sunset. All day they'd ridden slowly, covering maybe a third of the distance they had yesterday. They stopped for the night on a sage-dotted flat where they could make a fire between sheltering boulders. Nothing at all was said; the two older men slumped on the ground, and Jason went about the camp tasks.

Heath was feverish, his eyes too bright, his brain still calculating. He broke the silence with a quiet taunt. "You haven't done well today, old man. You've pushed too hard and it's catching up. Perhaps so will my friends before long."

Penmark's gaunt head lifted. "If they do catch up," he said softly, "you're a dead man. No matter how it goes, you're dead."

"Mm, yes. You know, I was afraid of that."

Heath rolled a dead cheroot between his lips, dryly chuckling. He had more cold guts than Jason had ever seen, but it wasn't likely to do him a jot of good. Let it develop he might be rescued and Penmark would shoot him like a dog.

Penmark had a reserve of savage strength he kept digging into; even tired and beat-out, dulled by grief, he hadn't reached the end of it. He put me down for sure, Jason thought, but I don't feel put down noways. Penmark's bereavement had festered in some way that was turning him strange. You couldn't hate that or even resent it much. If it made him dangerous in a way, you felt it as an impersonal kind of threat, like a coiled rattler: keep out of its way and it would leave you alone. Only that might be hard to manage. If their plans for Heath clashed again . . .

They ate the slight fare of coffee, bacon, and cold biscuits. Then it was full dark, and a wind was rising from the south, tattering the fire. Brush rattled and a coyote called somewhere. Jason said, "Sir, you want to split the watch same as last night?"

Penmark sat by the fire, a blanket around his shoulders. He seemed to be half-dozing, and now, abruptly, he raised his head. But he didn't even glance at Jason. He was hard-faced alert, listening. Suddenly he stood up, shedding the blanket, and kicked sand on the fire. Jason fumbled up his rifle, listening now.

Penmark spoke then, to Heath and very quietly, "You let one peep out o' you and it'll be the last thing you know."

44

"Mr. Penmark?"

"Shut up, boy. Keep your eyes open. Watch."

Jason sank down on his haunches among the rocks. For a straining moment he couldn't make out a thing. Remembering an old warning by his father that a man who stared into fire was momentarily blinded when he looked away from it, he'd been careful not to watch the flames. Now, in the wipeout of fireglow, his eyes quickly accustomed themselves to the surrounding dark. It wasn't total; starshine lay faint on the flats and ridges, frosting the gray-silver bunches of sage.

He picked up the sounds first: a creak of leather, a stir of bit chains. The noise carried at an angle against the wind. Isolating its direction as westerly, Jason quickly saw the dark shapes of riders coming slow through the starlight. Two of them, he thought. And a third horse, a pack animal.

"Hellooo, the camp!" a man called. "Friends here. Can we come in?"

"Who are you?" Penmark said harshly.

"Our name's Jamison. On our way from the Pana-mints. We spotted your fire as she was coming dark. All right if we ride in?"

"You be slow about it."

They gigged their horses forward. Halting a few yards away, the lead rider stepped to the ground. Jason couldn't see his face well, but he was slight and moved stiffly, and his right arm was held at a crooked angle from his body. The other rider got down too, muttering "Goddam." A woman's voice, and her heavy skirt had

45

got hung up on the pommel. She jerked it free, swearing again.

"We're with folks again," the man told her in a dry, mild voice. "You be watching how you talk."

"Surest thing you know, Pappy."

"Nothing like a she-pup for sass," the man said mildly. "Listen, we don't want to horn in on nothing here."

Penmark was on his feet, legs braced apart; his rifle was up and ready. "Depends what you want."

"Well, some of that coffee I smell would go good."

"Build up the fire, boy." Penmark spat sideways. "What you been up to in the Panamints?"

"What I do mostly. Hunt gold. We got a pokeful if you want to look."

"Heading where?"

"For Bodie over west, where the assay office is."

"You picked quite a time for it. There's hostiles out this way. Cayetano's Cherry-cows."

"Jehosephat. We didn't know that. Have been back in the Panamints a good month. Let's see, this here's Saturday, yeah, month tomorrow it's been."

Jason worked the fire up and fed sticks into it till the leaping blaze picked out the newcomers clearly.

They looked tired and dirty and worn. Jamison was a kind-faced man with eyes like smooth pebbles; the hair burred white around his temples under a slouch hat. His crooked right arm had a shrunken look and was probably useless. His daughter was on the short side, kind of, but not small exactly. She filled out her faded

46

duck jacket like the girls you saw pictured on bourbon labels and harvest-time posters and the like.

"I'll have a look at your plunder," Penmark said, motioning at the packhorse. "Throw it down."

"You know, I'd say you're almighty skittery."

"You'd be right. Throw it down and spread it out."

Jamison undid the pack hitch and dumped the whole load to the ground. He nudged the pack open with his boot and scattered its contents some. There were tools for prospecting, all right, and they had seen hard use. Penmark said he'd have a look at the poke mentioned. Jamison dug it out from a deep pocket of his tattered blanket coat, opened the drawstring mouth, and palmed a little of the dust.

"Take a good look, mister. Ain't none o' your low-down pig gold. That's . . ." A slow worry creased his face. "Listen, you boys ain't road agents, are you?"

"Just so you ain't. Put your gold away. You can spread your traps here if you're a mind."

"Thankee." Jamison tilted his chin at Heath. "Him . . . what's he tied for?"

Penmark made a meager explanation while Jamison tended to their animals and the girl set about fixing grub. Jason kept trying not to watch her. Only girls he was used to were his sisters, and neither of them had such free and bouncy movements. He figured this Jamison girl was older than his older sister Gayla Sue, who shaded Jason by a year. Maybe three or four years older. Gayla Sue was generally figured for a looker, but Sue didn't have coppery hair with bronze glints in it or eyes that snapped with greenish sparks. This Jamison girl was surely made to take a man's eye. Heath seemed appreciative.

"What's your name, my dear?" he asked.

"None of your business."

Jamison paused in lighting a stubby pipe. "Christine, you be minding your manners around folks. I ain't going to say it again."

"Good."

He pursed his lips around the pipestem, shaking his head "I got to tell you men it is no light thing to raise a woman-child the way I live. Had us a little place on the Brazos, but after Christy's ma, rest her soul, took the milk sickness and passed on, I went back to gold-finding again. It is a lonesome way to live, and I fear no life for a budding woman. She has taken on a lot of bark, which I am of a mind to larrup off."

"You try it once," Christy said.

"Think you're too old for a hiding, do you?"

"Damn right I am. You try it."

It was strange-sounding talk between them, yet somehow so casual that you got the feel they were merely talking across one another's head for amuse-ment. But people living off in lonesome places were likely to get so, Jason supposed. A little dotty.

Heath showed his teeth pleasantly. "Would you do me a kindness, my dear? Bring me a drink of water?"

"You stay away from him, girl," Penmark snapped. "That man's a killer."

"He is?" She sat on her heels by the fire, stirring

48

crackers and canned tomatoes together in a skillet. "Who'd you kill, mister?"

Heath laughed. "My dear girl, life kills each of us in its own way. Soon or late, quickly or slowly. Pumps you full of ideals and then grinds the ideals to powder. However we reach it, the grave's our goal. Most I've ever done for one or two chaps, a favor really, was given them a premature nudge that way."

"Do tell." She sounded totally indifferent. "Fetch me that slab of bacon from the pack, Pappy."

"Fetch it yourself." Jamison was seated comfortably tailor-fashion by the fire, facing Penmark across it. "You got better legs than me."

"Thanks." She rose to her feet and went to the pack where they had dumped it, crossing behind Jason where he was hunkered, so close that her skirt brushed his shoulder. " 'Scuse me . . . ."

At the same moment Jamison cleared his throat loudly, then laid down his pipe and reached his bony left hand inside his blanket coat. It came out holding a .44 Dragoon Colt, which he cocked and leveled at Penmark's head. "Now then, mister. You leave your hands where they be. Sit tight and don't wink an eye. Or I'll blow your head off your shoulders."

Jason's hand twitched toward the rifle he'd laid at his side. A ring of cold steel jammed against the back of his neck, and the girl said quietly, "That goes for you too, boy. Hold still."

Penmark sat with his legs folded, rifle across his thighs. He stared at Jamison through the fire, its glare rippling. across his gaunt face. His hands were resting on the Winchester, and for an instant they tightened there. He would be dead, Jason knew, before he could bring the piece up. . . .

But Penmark was unmoving then, and Jamison nodded. "That's wise. Christy, I'll watch the young-un too. You pick up his gun, then come get the old man's."

Heath's shoulders jerked with laughter. "Well done, Dallas. But what took you two so damned long?"

IV

After he'd cut Heath free, the old man called Dallas whacked some short lengths off a reata and used them to tie up Jason and Penmark, binding them hand and foot while the girl Christy casually held her pistol on them. It was a snub-nosed little Allan that she'd easily carried on her, bringing it out as soon as she'd moved back of Jason. He felt sick with chagrin at how easily the two of them had managed it, bluffing their way into the camp and smoothly putting Penmark and him off their guard. One simple coordinated move and they were masters of the situation. But who'd have guessed an old prospector and his daughter to be allies of Heath?

"Jamison," muttered Penmark. "Jamison, hell. You're Dallas Redmile."

Dallas grunted as he jerked Jason's hands tight behind his back. "Hell, mister, I know who I am." His voice was still mild and tired, but his crooked arm

50

wasn't entirely useless; it was aiding his good one. "That'll do 'em, Jack. They're trussed like a pair of prize hogs."

"Good. Christy, have a look at this leg of mine, will you?"

"Surest thing you know, honey."

The girl dropped the pistol into her jacket pocket, went to Heath, and kneeled down to work off his boot. He leaned back on his elbows, gently rolling the cheroot between his teeth. "I take it Miguel reached the rendezvous at least."

Dallas grunted. Hunkering down by the fire, he scraped some of the bubbling tomato and cracker mess from the skillet onto a plate and began eating hungrily, talking between mouthfuls. As Jason got the sense of it, the wounded Mexican had gone straight to Arrowhead Tanks where the gang was to rendezvous. Dallas and Christy, apparently the only members of Heath's pack who hadn't taken part in the robbery, were waiting there for Heath and the rest. Pure luck, Dallas observed, that the Tanks weren't far away from where Heath had been captured. Miguel had gotten there about midnight. Driving a hard pace, he'd lost a share of blood and was pretty weak, but had enough left to make clear what had happened.

It had left Dallas and Christy with the choice of waiting for other members of the gang to show up or of undertaking to rescue Heath on their own. Any delay might stretch it too fine, they'd decided, and trying to take him from his captors by outright force

51

might get him killed. A simple ruse had seemed the best way. Dallas had his prospecting tools and poke of gold dust: equipment he'd used as a cover for his identity when, somewhat over a week ago, he'd gone to New Hope to reconnoiter the town and particularly its bank for the upcoming job. The same masquerade might enable them to trick Heath's captors without endangering his life. This morning he and Christy had backtracked Miguel to the valley where Heath had been taken, picking up the trail north from there. Having fresh animals, they'd overtaken Heath and his captors by sunset, after which they had simply swung up on this camp from the west, as if bound from the Panamints.

"Very good—" Heath grimaced as Christy unwrapped the caked and filthy bandage around his swollen leg. "Damn it, my dear, go easy there."

"Sorry, honey. Maybe I'd better soak this off."

"Do it then. How is Miguel?"

"He be all right," Dallas said, reaching for the skillet again. "We left him resting comfortable, food and water to hand. You hanker for any of this chef's delight, daughter, or can I finish 'er?"

Christy made a sour face. "You can shampoo with it for all I care, Redmile. But please, no more of that daughter crap, all right?"

Dallas's smooth-pebble eyes twinkled with sly lights. "Anyways, you ain't stepping out of character. Good girl."

Their banter suggested a wry affection between these

two, even if the father-daughter thing had been a sham. Dallas Redmile's place in Heath's outfit seemed obvious: crippled and past his prime, he could still turn an old-lobo shrewdness to good advantage where any subterfuge was needed, thanks to an unimpressive appearance and colorless manner. But what about the girl? Maybe the answer was in the gentle care with which she set to sponging Heath's leg. Tender shades of concern chased across her face, which tightened to a quick anger as she finally peeled away the bandage.

"My God, look at it!" She stared at Jason and Penmark. "You bastards don't believe in coddling anyone, do you?"

Heath laughed. "Don't be too hard on them, angel. These are men of tenacity and conviction. Who, as it turns out, have busted their asses, in the argot, for exactly nothing. I almost consider my score with them evened. Dallas, old curmudgeon, I hope you thought to pack along a drop of firewater on this errand of mercy."

"Y'bet."

Dallas produced a bottle from his saddlebag, pulled the cork with his teeth, and took a long swig before passing it to Heath, who drank and shuddered. "Well now, that's pure rotgut at least. Undiluted by quality. All right . . . we stay here tonight. Tomorrow we'll pick up the loot, then be on our way to Arrowhead Tanks."

Dallas stroked his chin. "How far we got to go? Miguel mentioned you hid the money a ways out of Corazon."

Heath nodded. "Seemed a reasonable precaution, slowed as we were by poor old Artie. Matter of fact, we're not far from the place now. Just a matter of swinging a few miles west of here . . . ."

Christy's mouth compressed; she shook her head. "This leg needs attention. You ought to stay out of the saddle a couple days."

"That's fine, angel, but I'm afraid the situation won't permit any luxury of delay. To clarify things a bit—" Heath pulled at the bottle again and wiped his mouth reflectively. "These two chaps were part of a sizeable posse which split up after we did, putting several men on the trail of Miguel and Artie and me, others after Pete Ermine and Cherokee, still others trailing the other two Ermine boys. But all our friends, I'd guess, shook pursuit rather easily, thanks to their spare mounts. While Miguel and I, delayed by Artie slowly dying on our hands, were finally overtaken by the pair yonder. Who apparently had better reasons for sticking to a long chase than did some erstwhile companions of theirs."

"So all them others likely give up by now," Dallas said.

"More than likely. The original posse was hastily formed, badly provisioned. With food and water low, horses tiring and easily distanced by our men, I'd say we can count them out as of a couple days ago." Heath paused. "Thing is, though, a woman was accidentally killed in the shoot-out at New Hope . . . ." He motioned at Penmark with the bottle. "That old boy's wife."

"Jesus," Dallas said quietly. "A woman-killing. That's a damn sorry piece of business, Jack."

"I couldn't agree more, old pal, but it's done. And it's a sure bet that the sheriff's office at Longworth, the county seat, will be setting up an organized search for the dastards who are responsible. They'll telegraph word all over the territory. We could become the focus for quite a manhunt."

"We was heading for Mexico after the job anyways."

"Right. But with all due haste now. Let's assume that Cherokee and the Ermines have arrived at rendezvous or will shortly. Miguel will inform them as to what's happened. They might follow you and Christy, but chances are they'll wait awhile. We'll pick up the whole crew at Arrowhead Tanks and be on our way to the border. Miguel and I will have to manage as well as we can."

Dallas tipped his head toward the prisoners. "Them?"

Heath turned a cold measuring glance on Jason and Penmark. "We'll see," was all he said.

Breaking camp at dawn, they set out westward toward the outline of a monumental ridge where Heath said he'd cached the bank loot. Rocking in his saddle, Jason was blinking and crusty-eyed; he'd spent a near sleepless night wondering what Heath had in mind for them, feeling with a chill certainty that the man was capable of putting them both out of the way without thinking twice about it. On the other hand, Dallas had argued

55

hard against it, and Christy had added a few equally hard words. Why not set the pair of 'em afoot? By the time they reached a settlement, the whole gang would be safely in Mexico. Heath, tight-mouthed with irritation, had merely repeated himself: *"We'll see."*

Heath was riding in the lead, his powerful body erect. Christy had spent half the night putting hot packs on his leg to draw the first sign of infection. The treatment seemed to have done its work and he was holding up well. Jason, parched and miserable, jogged along behind him. Both he and Penmark rode with hands lashed to their pommels. The pace was jolting and brutal over this broken terrain, and Jason could feel his wrists being chafed to a raw agony. Dallas and Christy and the spare animals brought up the rear.

The sun was high, turning the rocky scape to a sullen furnace, when they halted at the boulder-strewn base of the crumbling ridge. Heath dismounted and limped over to a good-sized rock, which he heaved aside, exposing a shallow pit. He pulled out a pair of bulky saddlebags, tossed them over his shoulder, and walked back to his horse.

"All right, Dallas. You can cut these two loose."

"Sure I can," Dallas said dryly. "Then what?"

"Then I'll give 'em what they wouldn't give me. A chance to walk out of this desert alive. Walk, mind you."

"Without grub or water?"

"Give 'em a canteen of water, just one." Heath toed a foot into stirrup and swung up painfully to the saddle, his jaw set with pain. "As for food, let 'em make do. Bodie's the nearest settlement, and they ought to make it in three days." He gave Penmark a mildly relishing grin. "You can find the place, can't you, old pot?'

Penmark was hunched in his saddle, and he raised his head slowly, staring straight at Heath. The deep-socketed eyes smoldered in his haggard face; he didn't say a word.

"You can leave us our guns," Jason said out of a dry throat. "You can do that anyways."

Heath's acid grin twitched wider.

"Listen, those 'Paches who hit Corazon was swinging west. We get caught on foot, two men alone, we wouldn't have no chance."

"Miserable prospect, isn't it? No chance. I know the feeling."

"Jack . . ." Christy nudged her horse over by him. She was seated astride, skirt bunched around her legs, and she handled the raw-boned sorrel with an easy hand. "Let me ask you something. Did you ever pull wings off flies when you were a kid?"

"Going on the prod a bit, aren't you, Christine?"

"You bet your sweet ass I am." Her chin and jaw hardened to one smooth line. "Either you're giving these two a chance to live or you're not. Which is it going to be?"

A sleepy amusement touched Heath's smile. "Why, it's going to be whatever tickles your fancy, my dear. Not a whit less." Hipping around in his saddle, he pointed southward, glancing at Jason. "You see that

57

spire of red sandstone about a mile from here?"

Jason nodded.

"We'll leave your guns there. I'd wait till we're out of sight before I'd start after them. Be a pity if you chaps were too near us when you get weapons in hand again. I'd suggest, therefore, that you not be in too much of a hurry . . ."

They watched the three ride away, each of them leading some of the extra animals. As soon as a crest of land cut them off from view, Penmark began tramping after them.

Jason trudged behind him, the day's heat already dragging at his heels. But Penmark appeared gripped by another surge of that implacable energy of his. He walked erect and tireless, never glancing back or aside, never saying a word. Both men were wearing cowman's half boots. Not the best footgear in the world for a long hike, Jason thought morosely.

"Sir, how far away is this Bodie?"

"Like he said, hoofing it, about three days."

"I surely hope you know how to get there."

Penmark glanced contemptuously over his shoulder. "Jesus. Be in a dandy fix if I didn't, wouldn't you? We hoof it up to Corazon, then follow the stage road west."

"You reckon we can make it on one canteen?"

"There's water at Corazon. There's Red Jack Springs between there and Bodie. Red Jack don't never run dry. Be water enough to see us through."

The grim hardness of his voice didn't change, and

58

Jason said hesitantly, "What about when we get to Bodie?"

"Me, I'm getting me horses and a good outfit and I'm coming back. You do what you want."

Jason didn't reply, but the idea seemed hopeless to him. Heath and his companions would have pulled a far lead by then, be reunited with the rest of their gang and on their way into Mexico. Why take up the chase again? They'd lost Heath and the money—it looked like for good—and supposing they did find him again, they'd face impossible odds.

It meant nothing to Penmark, of course. He wanted revenge, pure and simple, and his own life was of no account to him. But Jason wasn't obsessed, only bitterly disappointed that he'd maybe had his bird in hand, only to lose it. He had failed his family for whose welfare he, as its remaining man, was now responsible. Failed himself too, in an obscure way he couldn't quite define. Except that making good at recovering or replacing what had been taken from them had begun, somehow, to resolve itself in his mind as a testing of his manhood. That was the real blow of failing on the edge of success.

Yet, considering it realistically, he'd done all that might reasonably be expected. No cause to feel disgraced. Fact, Ma and Gayla Sue and Josie, worried sick over him by now, would scold hell out of him for foolishly risking his neck far as he had. Privately proud of him maybe, but genuinely scolding too. And with the three of them dependent on him, he had no business risking the neck in question any further . . .

They reached the spire rock.

Scanning to the south, Jason found no sign of Heath and his two friends anywhere on the baking and broken scape. They'd been here and gone on, leaving the guns—both of their rifles and Penmark's Colt .45—in plain view on a flat stone. And something else that was welcome, a sack of jerked meat. Likely Christy's doing. It was her influence with Heath and not Dallas's, as Jason now reckoned, that had accounted for their lives being spared.

Heath couldn't have many such soft spots. He was hard and ruthless and clever, and he talked like he had a tall jag of learning. Jason wondered more and more about him, and about the girl Christy.

Again the two men tramped northward. Jason's feet were starting to pinch and hurt; he could only guess at how long he might keep up this steady hiking. It wouldn't matter to Penmark, who would wear his legs to bloody stumps if he had to.

By the time they reached Corazon around noon, Jason was gritting his teeth against the pain that shot into his calves. He wanted to rest, but Penmark hadn't once slacked the severe pace he'd set. In light of Penmark's oft-voiced opinion of him, keeping up with the older man had become a matter of bitter pride for Jason.

Penmark had no intention of resting now either. They paused at the Corazon well just long enough to replace the water they'd consumed from the canteen. Jason couldn't stand to look at the three corpses, what remained of them, and the stench was horrible. The bloated carrion birds didn't bother to take flight, but merely flapped and waddled off a few yards from their stinking feast. He fought down an impulse to shoot at them. The buzzards were doing the work that lack of Christian burial made necessary. He was relieved when the two of them had left the place and were continuing west along the hard-rutted stage road, the sun clean and hot on their faces.

About an hour later Penmark did concede a halt, wordlessly dropping on his haunches in some rock shade. The two sipped from the canteen and slowly chewed a handful of jerky apiece. At last Penmark broke his long silence.

"Well, Drum, you decided what you'll do when we raise Bodie? If you're a mind to trail with me, I got money enough to outfit us both."

Jason tried to keep the shock of surprise from his reply. "Thanks. I don't reckon I will." He couldn't help adding, "Don't suppose that'll make you too sorry."

"I don't give a goddam one way or t'other what you do, boy. Had I aught against you siding me, I wouldn't a offered."

"Yes, sir. Thanks just the same."

Penmark was silent awhile, jaw-grinding a hunk of jerky to a fibrous pulp that would slide down his throat. Finally he said, "You done good enough. Sure-hell better'n any of them soft-bellied counter-jumpers we left New Hope in company with. You done good enough for a green hand."

Jason didn't know what to say; he mumbled something or other in reply.

Penmark stared down the dusty ribbon of road, scrubbing a palm over his whisker-furred jaw. "Can't gainsay giving up mightn't be good sense, way things are. Only I can't turn back. No reason to. You understand that, boy?"

Jason nodded. Penmark's tone hadn't softened by a jot; only his words implied a relenting of sorts. This might be the time, Jason reflected, to pursue his curiosity about the outlaws.

"Mr. Penmark, I wonder what you know about this Captain Heath. I never heard of him."

Penmark shrugged. "I know what's common talk anywheres in the territory. Kind you pick up around any campfire or saloon. What they say about Heath, he come of a rich family in Kentucky. Had him a good schooling in England, they say. Later went to West Point. Was there when the war busted out. He joined up with Tierney's Raiders. Bunch of Southern 'cotton aristocrats' who formed an irregular regiment to fight Yankees their own way. No discipline from above. As the war dragged on, the lot of 'em begin to turn crazy mean. Took to raiding settlements on both sides. Burning, looting, and worse. Jeff Davis outlawed Tierney's guerrillas early in '65, and it was Confederate troops who run 'em down and wiped 'em out."

"I heard of that."

"Hell, every schoolboy has. Young Jack Heath and a few others got away and fled to Texas. Heath been

62

mixed up in a lot of shady dealings since. Has turned his hand to everything from hustling wet cattle across the border to knocking down trains and banks. That military training of his allus shows. Way he scouts out a place or has some'un else do it. Organizes everything to the nines. Provisions, spare horses, emergency tactics. Like timing this steal for when Cayetano is got near everyone in the country laying low. Like splitting up his force as he done out of New Hope. That's Captain Jack Heath, what I heard of him."

Penmark paused, tearing off another piece of jerky with his teeth.

"Uh, those others—"

"Redmile, he's an old-time high-grader in these parts. Spent him some time in Yuma Prison. I have heard his name coupled with Heath's now and then. The dead one, Artie, I never heard of. But they're all cut of the same cloth. Them others Heath mentioned, there's Cherokee, he's a half-breed, mean bastard with a knife they say. The Ermines, they're Trask Ermine, a guntipper of some note, and his brothers Pete and Clayt. Try keeping your eyes and ears open sometimes, boy. Way you learn."

"I expect so. I been stuck pretty tight to our place, you know, since we come to the territory. Ain't had a lot of chance to get out and around."

Penmark grunted, tilting the canteen to his lips.

"About that girl, sir . . ."

"What about her?" Penmark swirled some water in his mouth and spat it out. "World's full of female trash like that. Heath's doxie, not his first. Find his kind any-where, you can bank her kind won't be far away. Fit together like hand and gloves."

"Mr. Penmark, it is my reckoning she likely saved our lives. You got to give her that."

Penmark lowered the canteen, his eyes bleak as flints. "Boy, one thing you'll learn before you get a sight older, there's two kinds of women in this world. Just two kinds. You get lucky at all, you will meet up with a good one. A man can't ask for no better in life."

His voice had dropped to a whisper, tight and cold and bitter. Abruptly he rose to his feet.

"Time we got moving. Should raise Red Jack Springs about sundown by my figuring . . ."

V

Sundown. Jason hardly knew when it came. Dazzling heat rocked his eyeballs; he could hardly feel his feet or legs any longer. The rubbery stabs of sensation that remained were barely enough to keep him from reeling off balance. Penmark was starting to limp from his own relentless pace. And Red Jack Springs, Penmark had said, was located only a third of the distance to Bodie! Jason muddily wondered what good it would be having sufficient water when it was probable that by tomorrow the two of them would be too crippled up to continue on.

He almost lurched into Penmark, who had come to a sudden halt. Blinking his eyes clear, Jason saw a broad oasis of scattered cedars lined against the grainy pinkish glow of the last sunrays.

"Are we there?" His voice croaked out, shocking him.

"Yeah. So is someone else."

Jason blinked again. Now he spotted a ragged plume of smoke rising from somewhere in the trees. "That ain't? . . ."

"It's a white man's fire." Penmark ducked his tongue disgustedly. "Maybe he wants to smoke himself up a pile of trouble. That's how to bring it. Let's go in, but slow."

They approached through the thin line of trees. Grass grew thickly underfoot, and the ground had a feel of damp seep-fed chunkiness. Jason saw a glimmer of water; it reflected the orange blaze of a good-sized fire. He saw a man's dark shape standing close by; light raced faintly along a rifle barrel as it swung up.

"Who is that?" the man called. "You out there—"

"White men," Penmark growled. "Hold still. We're friendly."

A second man climbed to his feet now and stood by the other, both of them holding their rifles half-lifted. Jason and Penmark hauled up several yards away, facing them across the fire.

"What you doing way out here 'ith no hosses?" one of them asked.

Penmark took his time about replying, sending his gaze touching slowly over the camp without moving his head. The men's gear, most of it new looking, was scattered carelessly about. There was a brush lean-to

65

with some rumpled blankets inside. Four horses were hobbled a ways back in the cedars. A coffeepot and a copper kettle bubbling with something that looked like a grayish stew stood askew by the fire.

"You see anythin' you like?" asked the man.

Maybe he meant it humorously. He was thin and middle sized with a balding saddle of sandy hair. A mesh of crow's feet radiating from the corners of his pale eyes gave him a slyly secretive look. His big horsey teeth showed completely when he spoke; one of them was solid gold.

"Nothing much." Penmark fixed him with that flat uncompromising stare.

"Heh heh heh," the man said. "Can't take a joke, hey? I'm Hub Quitlow. This here's my nevvy Lafe. We're fresh outen Bodie. Got newly outfitted there. Are goin' for the Panamints to prospect some, we are."

" 'Pache trouble don't raise your short hairs none, I see."

"Oh, the Cherry-cows, hell, they done been raiding way south o' here."

"Was," Penmark said. "They hit Corazon two day back. Wiped out the Mexes who run the station there. Looked like they swung this way after."

"Well, we ain't raised no 'Paches."

"Cory-zone," muttered the other man. His cloudy eyes brightened. "Mexes, huh? Say, Uncle Hub, mebbe that be where—"

"Yeh." Hub cut him off in a flatly tolerant way. "That be where we're gonna strike out for the Panamints from. That is sure enough right, Lafe."

Like the other'd been about to say something he didn't want said. Lafe grinned in a foolish kind of way that was accented by the cleft of a deep harelip. By far the younger of the two men, he was burly and round shouldered with hair like matted straw.

"Lafe, he is slow between the ears," Hub said by way of explanation. "My brother Newt's boy. Got the care of him when Newt passed along. Be pretty much lost, Lafe'd be, if not for some'un to see after him."

That was fairly obvious; there seemed no particular call for stressing the fact. You had the feeling that Hub Quitlow wanted to be sure his nephew's remark was shuffled aside. Penmark merely nodded indifferently and said, "Trust you got no objection to the pair of us laying over by these springs tonight."

"Why shoot no, cousin, it is a public road." Hub's gold tooth flashed. "You welcome to share our vittles iffen you're mind."

Jason sensed a stiff-held wariness behind the man's accommodating manner. There was something ratty and shifty about the pair despite the newness of their gear. But could be it was just their way. He'd seen men of the same clannish, strange-acting ilk before. Hill-country scourings of an older frontier that was vaguely Southern, inbred by generations of isolated living till the features of any one could top those of any other almost twinlike. It showed in these Quitlows.

"Come from Corazon, did you?" Hub was saying. "All on foot, hey? Fancy that. . . ."

Grass rustled among the darkening trees. A girl's slight form came limping into the spread of firelight. She stopped at sight of Penmark and Jason, gazing at them dumbly. Her thin arms were clasped around a bundle of sticks she must have been gathering.

"Jest drop the wood over here, honey." Hub grinned at them. "Lafe's woman. She's a dummy too, manner o' speakin'. Cain't talk noways. Cain't speak a word."

The girl hobbled over by the fire and knelt, easing her armload of wood to the ground. She was Mexican or Indian from the look. And she'd been ill used, that was plain. Her rag of a calico dress was torn in several places; her black hair hung in a dirt-matted tangle. A shiny bruise purpled one high cheekbone. She was a little thing, thin to gawky in a coltish, adolescent way, and Jason had the shocked realization that she wasn't over sixteen, maybe less. Her brown legs were dusty and scratched below her calf-length skirt; one of her huarache sandals dangled with a broken strap. After that one long stare at them, she kept her head meekly down.

"Dish up the stew, honey girl," said Hub. "These here gents be hungry."

"Not right yet," Penmark said gruffly. "Feet're in bad shape. Gonna soak 'em in that cold spring."

"Jest the thing," Hub grinned, "long's they don't pizen the water."

Lafe rolled his dull eyes and cackled. Jason moved after Penmark as the older man tramped slowly around the fire toward the springs. The girl's head lifted furtively, her dark eyes briefly locking his. Then they

68

fell away. Jason's spine began to crawl. He might have been mistaken as to what he'd seen in that first long look of hers. Now he was sure he hadn't been.

What he'd seen was fear. Naked and shining fear that—he was almost sure—mingled with a kind of dumb pleading. What did it mean?

Several saucer-shaped depressions where water pooled cold and fresh to the surface gave Red Jack Springs its name. Penmark eased down on his rump by one of these and proceeded to work off his right boot, grimacing with pain. "Goddlemighty, my dogs are swole all to hell. Be easier to cut the sons a bitches off . . ."

Jason plunked down beside him, muttering, "Mr. Penmark. There's something dead wrong here."

"That young'un, yeah. Something amiss with him for sure."

"I mean that girl. She is been harshly used."

Penmark grunted as he jerked his foot free of the boot. "Looks to be, all right. Sorry thing to see. But she is wife to a man, and he got whatever use of her it suits him. You don't meddle between a man and his wife."

"Supposing she ain't his wife?"

"Hell, his kept woman or whatever, then. Either way it's no mix of ours."

"Sir, that girl is plain-out scared. The way she looked . . . I never seen the like of it in a human face."

"Like you said, Drum, you ain't been out and around much."

Penmark had wrestled off his other boot and

removed the remnants of his socks. Groaning with relief, he sank his reddened feet into the water. "Ahhh . . . that's the ticket, by God. Get off your boots and soak your dogs. Feel a sight better, I'll tell you."

"Suppose—" Jason hesitated. "Suppose they are keeping her against her will."

"Reckon you can ask her."

"That Quitlow said she can't talk."

"Can't tell you nothing then, can she?"

Jason could no longer bite back his anger. "Damn you! Don't you care about anything?"

"Yeah," Penmark said softly. "One thing. I care about one thing, boy. I told you what that be. Now you hear me, Drum, and hear me goddam good." He fixed Jason with his dead graystone stare. "This situation is no mix of mine or yourn. You want to brace that pair over a miserable greaser wench, you do it alone. I ain't lifting a goddam finger. You hear me?"

Jason nodded dismally. Might as well try to sway a stone wall as Val Penmark. He ought to know that by now.

Bitterly he began tussling with his boots. When he plunged his bare feet into the water, its icy clasp almost made him yell. But the cooling relief then came close to chasing everything else from his thoughts. The two men scrubbed their socks clean and laid them out to dry. Afterward they hobbled barefoot back to the Quit-lows' fire. Hub and Lafe sat cross-legged with tin plates on their laps, spooning stew into their mouths as fast as they could.

70

"Sit yourselves and eat," Hub Quitlow told them genially. "Honey girl, serve these men up some o' this good stew. You boys ain't said your names."

"Val Penmark from up New Hope way. This here's Jason Drum, same place."

"New Hope, hey? You be a long ways from home." Hub got his words out between mouthfuls, some of the stew spilling down his chin. He sleeved it away, bending forward with a show of real or feigned interest. "And all afoot, hey? That be a caution. You meet with a mishap?"

Speaking in his terse way, Penmark told most of what had happened during the past four days. The girl, meantime, was dishing up plates of stew for Jason and him. When she handed Jason his, he met the high luminous shine of her eyes once more. Again he saw the stark animal horror that seemed to tunnel back into her soul. He stared down at his plate, his palms sweating against its warmth. God, a man couldn't just sit and ignore that nameless, silent plea. But what else could he do? He wasn't sure of anything except that the poor creature was gut-deep frightened. . . .

The dilemma sat in his belly like solid lead as he began to eat. The stew was a lumpy, tasteless concoction of dried meat and watery broth that was way undercooked. Penmark ate his share with unconcealed distaste, mouth puckered as though he'd bitten into a briny pickle. The two Quitlows called for seconds. When the girl had refilled their plates, they fed their faces with undiminished appetites, wiping off dribbles

71

on their filth-crusted sleeves. The sight by itself was enough to spoil a body's eating.

"Do tell, do tell,' Hub mumbled around a full mouth as Penmark finished talking. "Too bad about your woman. Buried a couple myself back in Tennessee. Say, you two got some tall walking ahead o' you yit, you know that?"

"We know," Penmark said in a clipped voice. "Wonder if you'd be interested in making a dicker."

Hub raised his sly pale eyes. "Dicker f'r what?"

"You got fresh animals and a new grubstake . . ." Penmark leaned forward with a sudden intensity. "I can use both, and straightway. If I can backtrack from here without delay, good chance I can overhaul Jack Heath in a day or so. He won't be looking for no pursuit this soon."

"That mought be a handy trade for you, cousin, but it 'ud leave Lafe 'n me short of hosses and vittles."

"I can make it worth your while."

"Uh-huh. Well, we ain't in no almighty rush, a course. Just we'd have to mosey back to Bodie to fetch us more hosses and what-not, and that be a sight o' bother."

"I'll give you five hundred dollars for a saddle horse and a packhorse and some of your grub."

Hub spooned up the last of his stew and laid his plate aside, rubbing his belly. "Well now, that has an uncommon generous ring to it. You got five hunnerd dollar on you?"

"I got fifty in greenbacks in a belt under my shirt.

72

Will get the rest for you later. You want, I can write a letter for you to give my lawyer. Case I don't come back alive, it'll serve as a codicil to my will, directing him in my own hand to pay you four hundred and fifty dollars."

Hub was already shaking his head. "No deal," he said affably. "A Quitlow don't bargain for no empty poke. It's cash on the barrelhead or nothing."

"Goddamit." Penmark's voice shook; muscle ridged along his jaw. "Don't you know when to trust a man?"

"Shoot, cousin, you trying to dicker on a busted chip." The gold tooth glimmered. "Fergit it."

Slowly, still staring at Hub Quitlow, Penmark settled back; his mouth twitched. "All right. All right then," he said softly.

"More stew cousins? No?" Hub smacked his lips. "'Y God, that 'uz prime eatin'. Honey girl, you fetch us some o' that coffee now."

The girl brought some tin cups and handed one to each man, then wrapped a piece of cloth around her hand and picked up the coffeepot and carried it over to Hub and Lafe's side of the fire. Hub shook his head. "I declare, girl, body'd think you was raised in a sty o' some kind. No proper manners atall. Them two yonder's our guests. You serve 'em first, *comprende?* You snap to with dispatch now, or Lafe, he's like to swat you one."

The girl came limping around the fire. Her hands were trembling so much that she had to grip the handle of the coffeepot in both fists to steady it as she poured

73

for Penmark, then Jason. Young Lafe began banging his cup on his empty plate, grinning a wide stupid grin.

"C'mon dummy," he chortled, "gimme some coffee. You best snap to with dispatch there, or I gonna swat you so *goddamn* hard. . . ."

The girl hurried around the fire, and Lafe held up his cup. She tilted the pot to pour, her badly shaking hands causing it to chatter against Lafe's cup. Some of the boiling brew splashed on his wrist.

Lafe let out a howl of pain. He scrambled to his feet, yelling, "Jeezus, looka there, Uncle Hub, what she done! Burned me all to hell! Goddam dummy—"

He turned on the girl, his meaty hand swinging back. More of a blow than a slap, it knocked her clear off her feet. She hit the ground on her side, the coffeepot jarring its scalding contents across one bare arm. She screamed. Lafe's pink face split in a distorted laugh. The girl lay huddled as she'd fallen, moaning with pain.

Jason's right hand had already closed on the rifle by his knee. Now he lifted it to his thigh, holding it pointed down but ready.

"That's enough," he said tightly. "Don't lay a hand on her again."

Lafe quit laughing. His jaw hung open. Hub Quitlow's mild eyes began to harden and narrow. He picked up his own rifle and climbed slowly to his feet, holding it cradled on one arm. Jason matched the movement, getting up at the same time.

"My nevvy is troubled in his head," Hub said. "You

74

don't hard-mouth a troubled man that way."

Penmark laid his plate aside and rose too, uncoiling like a big snake. Jason snatched a glance at him, but Penmark was quietly studying the two Quitlows. His stance was relaxed, his face expressionless. He said nothing at all, as though he were letting the rest of them determine the next move. But in that instant, Jason knew that Penmark would back him.

"You best say your pardons," Hub said softly. "Then you pack out o' here, the both o' you."

"We're taking that girl with us," Jason heard himself say.

Hub's eyes half-lidded. "Young'un, you're twisting a wildcat's tail. You talking about another man's woman."

"I say you're a liar." The blood was pounding in Jason's ears. "A man don't use his wife the way—"

Aroused to a sudden combative rage, Lafe broke his silence. A crazy light quivered in his eyes. "Jeezus!" he bleated. "You hear him? He comes sits by a man's fire and eats his grub. Then he tells him how to fetch his woman about—"

Bending over fast, he came up with his rifle, snapping the finger lever down as he brought it to bear. His face was twisted and snarling. Jason's Winchester was already level, his motions smooth and unthinking as he levered it and fired. The bullet slammed Lafe half-around.

No time for Jason to even begin swinging his attention to Hub; the older Quitlow's rifle muzzle was

75

already fixed squarely on him. But he never pulled off his shot. Steel winked in Penmark's fist as his hand slapped down and up. He fired. The slug's impact flung Hub backward like a broken doll.

Lafe was still on his feet, fighting to bring his rifle up again. His eyes blazed crazily at Jason. For a long moment Jason could only stand rooted as he was; then he began wildly to jack another shell into his chamber. But Penmark shot first. Lafe's snarling mouth dissolved in a crimson welter. He crashed forward across the fire, his body exploding a cloud of sparks.

Hub pulled himself up to his knees, blood pouring from his belly. He tried to lift his rifle and failed. The rifle dropped; and he stayed on his knees, hands clamped over his belly.

Deliberately, Penmark thumbed back the hammer of his .45.

Frozen by the sudden and senseless smash of violence, Jason found his voice. "Don't!" he yelled. "My God, you finished him! He'll be dead in a minute!"

"I think he will," Penmark said, letting his pistol off-cock. "Well, I didn't think you had it in you, boy. But reckon you'd a been in a pretty fix if old Val Penmark hadn't took a hand in this ruction you started."

Penmark was, Jason saw with a shock, as near to smiling as he'd ever seen him.

VI

Jason spoke to the girl, making his voice quiet and gentle. She no longer seemed scared, but she was sure enough mute—quick-witted though, shaking her head and motioning at her mouth to indicate her lack of speech. He wondered if she'd been born that way or whether some mishap, or maybe scarlet fever, had taken her voice. The Quitlows had abused her, as the freshness of her bruises testified, but he couldn't be sure how badly. Anyway, she didn't have any crippling hurts, save for the slight limp.

Searching through the Quitlows' effects, he found a can of patent medicine salve. This he smeared on her scalded arm while she held it out. She understood everything he said all right, but he noticed she watched his mouth carefully as he talked, as if she had only a smattering of English. He asked her questions that could be answered by a nod or a shake of the head, but outside of ascertaining that no, she wasn't wife to Lafe Quitlow, he didn't learn anything that was helpful in regard to who she was or how she'd come into the company of this blue-ribbon pair.

Even if her hair were combed out and her filthy rag of a dress neatened up, he guessed she wouldn't be much to look at. Still, she was slender rather than bony, and had nice movements; she couldn't be over sixteen, and like his younger sister Gayla Sue, she was still teetering between girl and woman. Her face was thin and snub-nosed, but had less of an Indian look than he'd first guessed. With her dazed fear relaxed, he could see a fine structure to brow and cheekbones; her eyes were strong and expressive. She never took her gaze off him. Jason felt a growing embarrassment.

Hub Quitlow lay on the ground with his hands pressed over his belly, groaning, letting out a hard grunt of pain now and then. He rolled his eyes toward Jason. "Water," he croaked. "Water, please."

Jason shot a glance at Penmark who was crouched by the fire, examining Hub's rifle. "Forty-five Sharps," he murmured. "Telescope sight too." He raised it and lined his eye along the barrel. "Ain't that a dandy thing, though."

Again Jason felt a surge of weary disgust, but it was blunted by too much that had happened already. He didn't reply. No point saying anything to a man who was impervious to plain talk. Tiredly Jason filled a tin cup with water and kneeled beside the dying Quitlow, lifting his head and tipping the cup to his lips.

Hub had a hard time getting the water down, and his body gave a wrench of pain at each swallow. It wouldn't do him any good, all torn up inside as he was, but it couldn't make any real difference either. His eyes were dimming, the color graying out of his face.

"Bless you, boy," he whispered. "God bless you."

"There ain't nothing I can do," Jason said. "I'm sorry."

Hub began talking faintly. The words were disjointed and faltering, and Jason had to bend his head to catch them. What sense he could piece together from Hub's mutterings was that the Quitlows had found the girl this morning. She'd been wandering along the stage road in a daze, apparently headed for Bodie. They hadn't been able to fetch a word out of her. Anyway, Lafe had taken a shine to her, being full of sap and vinegar, his cub fancies easily tickled, and it hadn't seemed no harm letting him have his way, seeing the girl was just a greaser. . . .

Jason eased the man's last moments as well as he could. Then Hub was gone, and there wasn't a thing more to be done but the burying. Jason dumped out a pack that held the Quitlows' prospecting tools so he could get at a shovel. He wrestled out the residues of his gutted anger and disgust by tying into the flinty ground, forcing his rubbery muscles into motion as he widened out a double grave. Then he wrapped the bodies in a blanket apiece and laid the Quitlows side by side and covered them.

Finished, he straightened up, shuddering and sweat drenched, and met Penmark's cold stare. The older man sat cross-legged, Hub's rifle across his knees. "Good thing you got a strong back to go with your weak head, Drum," he said mildly. "You do like planting folks so damn much."

Jason's aching hands tightened around the shovel. He tramped over to Penmark and stood above him, swaying a little. Penmark didn't stir a muscle. "Like to lay into me with that, eh? All right, Salty, you think on just what happened here. You think on it a minute."

"Two men are dead, that's what—"

"Scum," Penmark said dispassionately. "A pair of low-down graybacks the world is better off shed of. Take it in their heads, they'd a killed you or me for a few dollars. Or no reason at all."

"They were men, damn you!"

"All right. I see I'm the one who's got to say just what happened. You started a ruction over that wench, and it got a couple men killed. You started it, Drum, but it took me to finish it." Penmark's lips pulled back till the flesh tautened skull-like to his jaws. "How you like it now, boy?"

Jason sat down and dropped the shovel at his feet. He looked at the girl as she wrapped a piece of cloth around her burned arm, her eyes still on him, and then he rolled his shoulders exhaustedly. "I don't know," he muttered. "Thanks for the help."

Penmark grunted. "What did he say?"

"Not a lot. They come on the girl this morning. Guess she was pretty much this way when they found her. All the same they used her rough." Jason's voice climbed a notch. "I done what had to be, Mr. Penmark. It was the right thing."

"Just so you're satisfied to that," Penmark said sardonically. "Now you got her, what you going to do with her?"

"Take her to Bodie, I reckon. Have a doctor look at her. No telling what's been done to her. Might be hurt some way we can't tell."

"You won't find no doctor in Bodie. What I heard,

it's a hardrock camp with a store, a saloon, an assay office, and nothing much else."

"Well, maybe she got some people there. Anyways, someone might know her. Who she is, where she's from."

"I hazard them dead Mexes back at Corazon could of told you."

"You think she come from there?"

Penmark beckoned to the girl. "You. Come over here."

Slowly she moved up by the fire. Penmark smoothed a patch of ground with his hand, then picked up a stick and marked a small cross in the dirt. "Corazon, *comprende?*" The girl nodded. He drew a line west from the cross, adding, "*Camino,* eh?" And marked another cross at the line's end. "Bodie, all right? You was heading for Bodie." Again she nodded. "*¿Donde vive?* You live at Corazon?"

Her face tightened; she opened her mouth. The tendons of her throat stood out as she tried to speak, but all she could manage was a kind of moan. She struck her mouth with the flat of her hand and fell to her knees, shaking her head back and forth.

Penmark spat into the fire. "Well, that says something. Seems she could talk before."

"Before . . . something happened?"

"Yeh. Could of got shocked speechless, I reckon. *That's* happened to folks."

Penmark talked quietly, forcing the girl's attention back. Her eyes followed the stick as he drew more marks in the dirt, at the same time putting further questions to which she could indicate yes or no. Bit by bit her story came out. The Apaches had come while she was off in the brush picking berries. It was almost over by the time the noise of a ruckus had drawn her partway back. Huddled in the brush nearby, she'd watched the tail end of the little massacre. Then the Apaches had fired the station and driven off the stock. She didn't remember anything after that except walking for a long time, till the Quitlows had found her.

Did she have live kin anywhere? People she could go to? She shook her head no, her eyes shifting between Penmark and Jason as if she expected them to have the real answer.

Penmark gave a disgusted grunt. "Well, that's 'bout it, boy. She'll be your lookout. Leastways I reckon that's how you'll want it."

"Ain't a question of what anyone wants," Jason said coldly, "it's—"

"Yeah, Christian goodness, I know. Ain't saddling myself with no greaser girl, that's sure."

"Then you don't need to worry about it, do you?"

Penmark shrugged. "I 'low to a hope you'd be inclined to trail 'long with me after all. There's Heath and I mean to get him. Am starting after him first light." A sudden twist of his hands snapped the stick. "I don't quit till I get that bastard. And this time I get him dead."

"Your business," Jason said in the same cold voice.

82

"I don't give a damn about Heath."

"Still give a damn for that money, don't you? You was itching after it fierce enough before." Penmark paused, his sated gaze locking Jason's. "We got horses now. And grub aplenty. Think about it."

Jason didn't reply right away. A dark suspicion had touched him, and now it ballooned full-blown in his mind. "Mr. Penmark. You said you wasn't going to take my part against these men."

"Hell, nobody in his right mind gets tolled into a ruckus that's no mix of his. But you had to push it."

"That ain't the point," Jason said thinly. "You wanted no part of it. That's what you said. Then you lent a hand anyways. You ain't gonna tell me you done it to save my hide."

"Ain't told you a damn thing of the sort, have I?"

"You don't need to." Jason hunched his body forward, taut on the balls of his feet. "That's why you changed your mind. With the Quitlows dead, you'd have their horses and grub. Then you could set straightway after Heath like you want."

"You're the one's saying it, Drum." Penmark's face was like a metal mask. "It don't make a damn lick of difference why I done it. I hadn't, you wouldn't be sitting up talking about it. And don't you forget it."

Jason bit back a hot reply. What good to argue with this man? He was hard enough, a man of his times. Yet like all such, he'd lived by deep-grained principles of his own, and his handshake was as good as his bond. The killing of his wife had snapped Penmark's iron code and swept the pieces away. All he cared about was getting the man he deemed responsible, Jack Heath. If Hub Quitlow wouldn't sell him horses, there'd remained one way to get them.

It had been, on Penmark's part, an act of simple murder. But if the man was no longer capable of seeing it that way, what could you say to him? Nothing. Particularly when it was sure as sunrise that Penmark, just as he'd said, had saved Jason Drum's skin. Whatever his reason, that cold fact couldn't be denied.

Penmark ended the long silence. "There's still the money. You don't argue what getting it back 'ud mean to you and yours."

"No," Jason said dully.

"Then you look at it that way, boy. You fix your mind to that and nothing else. We got the horses and the grub. Right now Heath got no more'n a day's lead on us. Thinking he's shed of all pursuit, he won't push too fast. We got that edge and another too." He leaned forward and tapped a finger on Jason's knee. "They won't be expecting us. We catch up before they raise the rest of Heath's crew, two of us can handle 'em sure. I'll have Heath. You'll have your money."

Jason gnawed the corner of his lip. Penmark's words held a cold persuasion that swayed him. The Quitlow horses, illgotten or no, put a fresh handle on the whole business. It was hard to thrust the temptation aside and shake his head.

"All right," Penmark said flatly, "there's the girl. What can you do for her she can't do for herself?

There's four horses. Gives us two saddle mounts and a packhorse. That leaves one animal for her. There's the road. All she got to do is follow it to Bodie."

"I aim to see she gets there safe," Jason said stubbornly. "I—"

A quick sound from the girl. She was motioning with her hands, shaking her head vehemently. She had followed enough of the talk to get its gist. No, she painfully made clear, she wasn't going to Bodie. A few questions by Penmark clarified what she intended to do: return to Corazon and bury her family.

Jason tried to argue her out of it, but he might as well have tried to talk down the wind. She held her mouth tight and kept shaking her head.

"Tough little beggar." Penmark's tone was touched by a bleak amusement. "You going back to Corazon with her, Drum?"

Jason gave a helpless shrug. "Seems I'll be obliged to."

"All right, then. I am going on Heath's trail by way of Corazon. You and her ride along that far. Give you time to think on it. Might just be you'll change your mind. Meantime, sleep on it." Penmark looked down at the rifle; his hand stroked along its barrel. "Yes sir . . . that is one dandy weapon for certain."

When he woke next morning, Jason was surprised to find it was past full dawn, the sun slanting bright against his eyes. He smelled bacon and coffee cooking and saw the Mexican girl already up and fixing breakfast—and was surprised all over when he saw Penmark still snoring in his blanket. It was long past first light. So pure exhaustion had finally overcome Penmark's iron determination and his impatience. Even he needed to rest sometimes.

It was the first real sleep Jason had known in days; he felt restored and finely alert. He went to the spring and took his time washing up. As he pitched into the meal the girl had put together, he found he was keenly hungry. They ate in silence, the morning pleasantly quiet around them, till Penmark roused out in a muttering, savage mood because he'd overslept. Stiff and haggard-faced, he gobbled down his breakfast while Jason and the girl saddled the animals and rigged up a pack.

They rode briskly east toward Corazon. Jason did a lot of thinking about what Penmark had said last night. Maybe it would be as easy as the older man thought, overtaking Heath's party and getting back that money. Heath was injured; his companions, an old man and a girl, weren't likely to offer a very tough resistance. Feeling chipper and renewed, Jason also felt his confidence stoking up, the fever of purpose gripping him again.

There was the Mexican girl, of course. That was the troublesome part. He'd been raised to a strict feeling in such matters. Man's part was to cherish and protect the distaff side. Plain conscience pointed to his proper course: see that she was gotten to a place of safety. But it would mean abandoning the pursuit for good, and that wasn't right either. He had an obligation to his own—who were on the distaff side too. He had no obligation at all to this little waif of a Mexican. Also, she was proving to be a sight tougher than her physical slightness would indicate. No reason she couldn't make it alone to Bodie, given a horse and supplies and a gun.

Danger? Odds that way cut pretty slim when you thought on it. The Apaches had made their swing across this territory three days gone; that threat was surely past. Wasn't much chance, either, of her meeting up with any others like the Quitlows. They had been the scum Penmark had named them; few Western men ever sank that low. No matter how hard a Western man of any stripe might be, he most always respected women.

By the time they came in sight of Corazon at noon, Jason had taken the fever of pursuit again. Penmark, who had neither youth's optimism nor its second saving strength, only a grim and driving impatience, motioned for a halt just before they reached the fire-gutted station. Hands crossed on his pommel, he looked bitter-eyed at Jason.

"All right, Drum. You had your time to think on it. What's it to be? You fetching up here or you coming with me?"

"With you. But I'm going to help the girl lay her kin to rest. It won't take long. You can ride on if you want and I'll catch up."

Penmark grunted sardonically. "All you do without

87

me alongside is get yourself lost. I'll help with the burying. Don't reckon there'll be a whole lot to lay away. . . ."

Digging a wide common grave was easy enough. The rest of it was the trying part, gathering up the carrion remains of three people and setting them in a proper order of sorts before filling in the grave. Jason had to fight his squirming innards through the ordeal and couldn't remember a feeling of relief as overwhelming as he knew when the job was over. He also felt an awed admiration for the girl, who had remained still-faced and contained through the whole business. She had refused to hold back, pitching in without a blink or a whimper beside Penmark and him until the last spadeful of earth had been patted into place.

While Penmark filled a small cask of water at the well and lashed it onto the packhorse, Jason talked haltingly to the girl, telling her he was going on with his friend and why. She listened carefully, then made some rapid gestures that he had a time making sense of. When he got her meaning, he shook his head vigorously.

"No, you can't come with us. That's out o' the question! You go on to Bodie. All you got to do is follow the stage road, understand?"

He felt foolish under her bright demanding stare; a slow heat washed into his face. "Look, that is how it's got to be. If you want, you can wait for us here. We will be back in a couple of days, about. Then I will see you to Bodie. You can go on alone if you want or you can

88

wait for me. But that is how it's got to be!"

A gritty wind flapped Anita Cortinas's ragged skirt around her legs as she stood watching the two gringos ride southward. She watched till they were only diminishing dots on the vast *playa*. Then she looked down at the freshly smoothed mound at her feet.

Kneeling beside it, she crossed herself and folded her hands on her lap. There was no priest to offer a committal prayer, to give the office of the dead, or say a Requiem Mass. She knew these things should be done, but of them she knew only what she had heard at one time or another. She had a mere gray memory of attending Mass in a white-washed village church when she was very small. 'Nita wasn't sure just where she stood in the matter of religion. It had never been a great thing with her father or mother, and *Abuelito,* her crotchety grandfather, had been very outspoken about believing in nothing at all. Voiceless, she couldn't utter a simple Hail Mary; even a silent prayer refused to shape itself in her mind. She couldn't weep, either, past the unyielding grief that knotted her throat.

Maybe it would all come later. The dazed numbness that had held her mind for so many hours had lifted. That was something.

She rose and brushed her hands over her dusty dress, then looked again after the two gringos. They were almost lost to sight now.

'Nita Cortinas was very sure of what she was going to do, though she barely knew why. Perhaps it was enough that she did not want to remain in this place, alone with a silent grave and the burned remains of her home. And somehow she did not want to lose sight of these two gringos. Maybe they would return, or at least the young one would, for he had said so. But maybe he would not.

Vaguely she thought of these two as a line to life: the only one, for now, that she knew. Here were only the dead and the memory of her last sight of them, to which she could not close her mind. For them, there was no more she could do.

She limped over to where the horse the gringos had left her stood in the shade of the station wall. Her right leg was still painful; she couldn't remember how it had gotten hurt. But she could get about on it; no bone was broken. The horse was a wiry paint mustang, who would bear her slight weight as far and as fast as the gringos' mounts would take them. The food and canteen and blankets that they had left with her would be little additional weight. Of these she made a small bundle, tying it to the saddle cantle. On the ground nearby lay a dirty piece of muslin, charred at the ends; picking it up, she recognized all that remained of some bolt goods from which her mother had planned to make a dress. Tucking in the ends, 'Nita wrapped the strip of cloth around her head and throat to shield them partly from the sun.

Holding the rifle in one hand, reins in the other, she essayed to climb into the saddle. She made it on the third try. Her skirt was hiked above her knees, and she spent a few awkward seconds trying to adjust the wide hem over her legs without much success. Afterward, she kneed the paint horse into motion and headed away from Corazon.

She did not look back.

VII

The country was a monotony of pinks and browns, largely flats that were stippled by silver-gray sage and broken up by sand-colored formations. A day of pushing steadily across it into more of the same wore Jason's eagerness back to a frayed nub. He wondered sourly why he always forgot that a body's moods pretty much depended on his general physical being, his digestion and the like; moods never lasted. One hour you were sitting on top of the world; next you were way down in the mouth. "Won't get no better as you get older, boy," Pap had once assured him. "You just take on more aches to plague you. It's in the way of nature, same as hot weather is and being tired is. Only them you learn to live with."

He guessed he had a sight to learn yet. Heat and weariness—the doses he had gotten on this trek were enough to last him a long while.

He and Penmark had backtracked to where they had split off from Heath's party yesterday morning, taking up the trail from there. Arrowhead Tanks, which had been mentioned as Heath's destination, where he was supposed to meet the rest of his bunch, was just a hop-skip from the line with Mexico, Penmark said. He didn't know exactly where the place was, but it was a well-known waterhole and a favored campsite of Indians. Anyway, it was at least a couple days' ride; with any luck they should come up on Heath and Dallas Redmile and the girl Christy before they got that far.

That was the important thing. Overhauling 'em before they reached the Tanks and were reinforced by the rest of their outfit. Odds against successfully taking 'em then would be impossibly steep. As it was, prospects seemed better'n fair. The Quitlow horses were tough Indian mustangs and were still fresh. Also the track showed that Heath wasn't pressing along fast. Chances of overtaking him by, say, early tomorrow looked good.

They made fair time all day; even Penmark was half-way satisfied when darkness forced them to halt and make camp in a narrow swale. They cooked some grub and sought their blankets, and were up before sunrise.

As they packed up and saddled the horses, Penmark was as edgy as a hunting dog: hot on the scent and keen to draw blood. "We be onto 'em by noon," he muttered, "or I miss my guess. . . ."

Jason merely grunted.

"Tricky part'll be when we take 'em. Depending on the lay of the land, maybe we can get 'em by surprise. We can't, it'll be rough. But either way, we are taking 'em right off."

Penmark cinched up his saddle, then stepped around

his horse and halted beside Jason. "One thing I want to get said so's there's no mistaking it."

Jason, frowning at his latigo, said "What?"

"You bucked me when we had him square in hand before. Don't do it again."

Jason nodded indifferently.

"I mean it. You try to stop me from fetching that bastard his just deserts, I'll bust you, kid. I'll bust you cold. You understand?"

"Uh-huh."

Penmark scowled. "What the hell's eating you now? We stand the best chance yet of getting your goddam money. What you want, ain't it?"

"I been thinking about that girl at the station. It wasn't a good thing we done, leaving her that way. Can't be sure she—"

"Jesus." Penmark shook his head; he was near to smiling for the second time. "I never see a good American boy sweat his balls over chilipickers like you do. That's something."

Jason took a step away from his horse and turned, squarely facing the older man. "Mr. Penmark, now I want you to get this. I heard all the talk of that sort I'm going to from you. If there is any more of it, you won't need to worry about us having a set-to over Heath. Next word you drop about greasers or spicks or chilipickers or pepperguts, we are going to have one right then and there. And it will be the damnedest ruction you ever walked into in your fifty-odd years."

Penmark eyed him a long moment, then nodded

slowly. "You taken some bark in your craw since we started out, ain't you? Just so's we understand each other. . . ."

As they rode steadily through a long morning, the monotony vanished in a keen stir of anticipation. Some of what Jason felt was plain nervousness, but he realized with a kind of detached surprise that he wasn't coming up skittish or queasy as had been the case before. No danger, this time, of his taking buck fever. What he felt more than anything was the high excitement of the chase, closing on their prey. No justifying the feeling; just now it was a good way to feel, that was all.

A little before noon, they spotted a tendril of smoke curling up beyond a tall and craggy-topped ridge. The two men looked at each other but didn't say anything. They pushed straight toward the odd-shaped promontory. When they halted a short distance from it, the smoke seemed pretty close, only the bald height of land cutting them off from its source.

Stepping to the ground, Penmark pulled the .45 Sharps that had belonged to Hub Quitlow from his saddle boot. Then he got out the telescope sight and his field glasses. As he fitted the scope sight in place, he said "About time we fell into some luck. That ridge is lucky for us. . . ."

"If it's them."

"Track goes straight on around the ridge. It's them. We got a prime chance to take 'em unawares, but I want a good sight on the layout first. Then we'll settle how we're going to handle it." He peered up at the ridge. "She's a good hard climb. I'll go up alone, you wait by the horses."

Jason hesitated. Penmark's state of mind bothered him; no telling just what he might do. Be wise to stick close to him. "Reckon I'll just go up with you."

Penmark gave him a raking glance, then turned on his heel and tramped away toward the ridge. Jason was right behind him.

The lower scarp of the rise wasn't too difficult to negotiate. It was sloped with ramps of crumbled rock that had weathered away and fallen from the upper height, forming a rough surface that could be climbed easily but slowly. They worked their way around the larger boulders, careful of their footing on the loose stuff. Had to be watchful of one's hand supports too, never touching one of the oven-hot rocks for more than an instant. Higher up, the formation grew quite steep, finally rounding off abruptly at its crown.

Both men were pouring sweat as they came onto the top, a sun-baked sprawl of blocky boulders and spires. The sun banked off the naked rocks with a furnace fury that beat at their bodies and rose through the soles of their boots. Not pausing, Penmark clambered over the rubble till he reached the shade of a giant boulder perched on the rim's south end. Moving up beside him, Jason saw that the ridge tipped off at their feet in an uneven, almost straight-down drop. It was forty or more yards to the bottom. From here they had a clear view of the sage flat that stretched away from it.

The huge rock was only middling warm in its pocket of shadow; pressed against its flank, they were merged with its shape, concealed from any but a close observer below. A good thing, for the camp wasn't over five hundred yards distant.

Jason made out six people ranged around a fire. Six? "Mr. Penmark, there's—"

"Shut up."

Penmark set his glasses to his eyes and studied the camp. Jason was tasting the brass-bitter significance of what the number of the party meant as, slowly, Penmark lowered the glasses.

"Seems their friends didn't wait at the Tanks," he murmured. "The Mex told 'em what was up and they come north following his back-trail. I hazard they just now met up with Heath, Redmile, and the girl."

"Mr. Penmark, there's only three of 'em."

Penmark rasped a hand across his jaw. "I never seen the Ermine boys, but that'd be them. Three gringos. Means the Mex stayed behind and I reckon that Cherokee, the breed, he did too. Well, it don't make much difference. Three and three makes six." He swiveled a wicked stare at Jason. "Means the odds have got a sight too steep. Only way to surprise that many 'ud be to sneak in close. Can't manage that on no open flat."

"Then there's nothing we can do."

"Oh yes," Penmark said gently. "There's still one thing, boy. There's Cap'n Heath." He patted the Sharps. "This old gun has the range. With a scope sight, be as easy as nailing a fish in a barrel."

96

Jason looked at him in disbelief. "Mr. Penmark . . . you do that, you will pull the rest of 'em right up here onto us. We never make it down this damn ridge before they cut us off."

"Think of that, now."

"Listen," Jason said heatedly, "you don't give a sorry damn about your own neck, all right! But it ain't all right you run mine into a noose too."

"I ain't about to, shorthorn. What you do, you get down off here and get clear away. Take my nag and the packhorse too. Time I let this gun off at Heath, you'll be good and gone." Penmark's mouth twisted faintly. "I'll give you time."

"Sir. Look." Jason blinked sweatily; he rubbed a shaking hand over his face. "If you won't think about your own life, think about this. You ain't even fired that Sharps, much less got it sighted in. This far a shot, you can't be sure. You just can't be."

Penmark palmed his watch in a quick gesture; he snapped open its case. "You got twenty minutes. Less'n that if they break camp and start to pull out before time's up. They do, I ain't waiting."

His voice was unchanging, his face still as stone. A peculiar shine had surfaced on his eyes. And Jason knew that the time for talking was past.

He turned and started away from Penmark, stumbling across the rubble toward the place where they'd ascended. Suddenly a shadow stirred in his path. Jason came to a dead halt, his heart almost stopping. Then he turned his head.

97

For a moment he didn't believe what he saw. A dark-faced man had stepped noiselessly from behind a leaning spire not five yards away. A short fellow, hard and squatly built, his black hair closely cropped to his head. His face was square and primitive under an old horse-thief hat. His strong scarred hands held a Winchester that was negligently aimed at Jason's chest.

Jason stood stock still, his muscles bunched with tension, as the man moved close, then reached out and took the rifle from his hands. For a wild moment Jason didn't know what to think. Then it came to him who this man was. Cherokee, the half-breed. He laid Jason's rifle on the ground, then made a tight menacing motion with his Winchester, indicating that Jason was to move back toward the rim.

Jason slowly wheeled and tramped back that way, his boots crunching on crumbled stone with what seemed an abnormal loudness in his ears. He knew Cherokee was right behind him, though the half-breed's moccasined feet made no sound.

Crouched by the big rock, Penmark was sighting along the Sharps as he drew a bead on the camp. Jason's throat tightened with the impulse to yell a warning. Then, hearing his footsteps, Penmark turned his head.

In the same moment the half-breed's rifle slammed into Jason's kidneys and knocked him sprawling. Penmark whirled to face them, moving away from the rock as he whipped the rifle around in a tight arc.

The crash of Cherokee's weapon came even as Jason

was skidding on his face in the rubble. Penmark jerked with the bullet's impact. Reeling backward, he toppled over the rim.

Jason, curled up with pain on the ground, had only a distorted glimpse of Penmark as he plunged from sight. A dim clatter of falling rubble followed. Then silence.

"Get up," Cherokee said.

Jason climbed shakily to his feet, half-doubled with the pain of his back. Cherokee jabbed him with the rifle, nudging him ahead, and together they moved over to the brink of the drop. A third of the way down its rough steep slant, Penmark's body lay hung across a projecting spur which had broken his fall. He was twisted and motionless, one leg hanging over the ledge. Blood dyed his gray hair and made a spreading brightness across the dust-colored rock where his head rested.

"I don't think he listen, that one," the half-breed said. "So then I shoot fast."

Jason looked at him.

Cherokee showed his strong yellow teeth. "Me, I'm sent up here for lookout. He don't take no chance, Heath. I see you and him coming long way off. I get out of sight and wait. Now you know, eh?"

The men down in the camp were on their feet, watching the ridge-top. One of them yelled something at Cherokee. In reply, the half-breed raised his rifle above his head and waved it once. Then he pointed it at Jason again.

"You go on down, boy. Stay ahead of me and go slow."

He retrieved Jason's rifle and brought it along. They clambered back across the crumbling top of the ridge and descended its sloped flank. Cherokee prodded him over to the three horses and told him to pick up the reins and bring them along. They tramped across the sage flat to the fire where Heath and his men waited.

Heath stood with his arms folded, holding his weight hip-shot away from his hurt leg. His pale stare held on Jason while Cherokee briefly explained what had happened. Afterward Heath's gaze moved to the low scarp where, from here, part of Penmark's body was visible along the spur rock.

"So he had to get me," he murmured, "and you had to get your money. Too bad. How did you come by the horses?"

Jason told him. Wasn't any reason not to. But he felt a cold dread even as he talked. Heath had ample cause to settle him too. Christy moved over to the leader and laid a hand on his arm.

"Jack . . . let the boy go, why don't you?"

"You know what, angel?" Heath said mildly. "I think the heat is scrambling your brains. Mine too, apparently. I let them go before on your say-so. I rather doubt the old man was drawing a bead on you or Dallas, up there."

"All right," she said coldly. "Go ahead and shoot him. While you're about it, remember he's the one who stood between you and the old man's gun before. Or so you told us."

Heath nodded bleakly. "True enough . . ."

"All he wants, from what you've said yourself, is to get his family's savings back. That right, Drum?"

"Yes'm."

One of the Ermine brothers rumbled a slow chuckle. About thirty, he was built like a great chunky wedge, tub-bellied but solid. His wreath of jowls sparkled with a burr of blond whiskers; his clothes were stiff with filth, and he gave off a sour aura of sweat and tobacco. His shirtfront was tracked with tobacco stains. He fired a squirt of brown juice at the fire now.

"Boy howdy, that's something," he said. "Maybe we oughta pat his rosy cheeks and give him back his money while we're about it."

"Not a bad idea," Christy said calmly, "considering the source. I'd say Jack owes him that. How much of your money we got, Drum?"

"Eight hundred—" Jason cleared his throat. "Eight hundred seventy-five dollars."

"Well, you do go for the big bucks, don't you? Jack, give him his money, it's a piddling piece of change we'll never miss. Then send him on his way. He won't bother us again. Will you, Drum?"

"No, ma'am."

The tub-bellied man shook his head, grinning. "Sister, you're something. You know that?"

"Careful what you say, Pete." Heath's voice had a warning edge. "Forget it, angel. This fellow's given me enough trouble, he and his friend. I'm taking no more chances with him. What we'll do, I think is take him along with us."

"Why?"

A flat, single word from the tallest Ermine brother. Just looking at this fellow, you got the feeling he never wasted speech. A raw-boned lath of a man in his mid-thirties, he wore his yellow hair long, curling over his collar. He had a bony clean-shaven face with a blade of a nose and eyes as chilly as Penmark's. A gaping pink scar that was six inches long laid open the side of his face; its edges had never healed together. The way he wore his gun, holstered at a jutting angle so that the wrist of his straight-hanging arm always brushed the butt, was what you noticed most.

"A hostage, Trask," Heath said. "A hostage to the border. I've been fetched enough surprises on this trip. Had thought we'd shaken his friend and him, and by God if they didn't show up again. I think Mr. Drum's presence might provide a splendid warranty against any more surprises."

"Thought you said we thrown off the rest of that posse."

"They all turned back, yes." Heath moved his weight to his stiff leg, grimaced, and shifted back again. "But word's gone out by now. No telegraph out of New Hope, but Longworth isn't too far from there. Longworth has wires to Bisbee and Tucson. From there word would be sent to the border. Of course there's not enough law down there to start to cover the whole

Mexican line, particularly where we'll cross. But as I say—I've had enough surprises this trip. Should we run into any more, Mr. Drum will be our passport."

"That makes sense, all right," Dallas Redmile said mildly.

"Shee-it," said the third Ermine. "Whatever be it Jack says, you go along, old man."

"So do you." Heath gave him that flat-edged look of his. "And don't forget it."

Clayt Ermine, this one would be. He was a lot younger than his brothers. Not much older than Jason, in fact. Callow-seeming and close-eyed, with Trask Ermine's blade nose, he was sort of a pale copy of his oldest brother. Held his lank body the same way and wore a jut angled Colt. But he dressed a lot fancier, wearing a costly looking calfskin vest and flowered sleeve garters. Under Heath's stare, a pale rage flared in his eyes, then veiled over with a thin caution. He remained fidgety as hell, and Trask gave him a warning look.

"All right," grunted Pete Ermine. "We all taken your orders right enough. Job's done and you still holding all the money. Time we made the split."

"That'll wait." Heath limped to the fire and swept dirt over it with his foot. "Right now—"

"Hell no, it won't wait," Pete said truculently. He set his hands on his hips, a massive hogshead of a man with no softness about him. "Suppose'n we got to break up again like we done out of New Hope. There we was kiting off in different directions and you had our shares. All right, it was needful, how you done it, posse hot on our asses and no time to divide the loot. But I don't see no odds we let that happen again."

"Well, well," Heath murmured. "I've rather a suspicion that Pete doesn't trust me. Could that be the case with all you bucko lads?"

Trask Ermine had the makings out and was building a cigarette. Not looking up, he raised one shoulder in a lazy shrug. "You never dealt a partner crooked that I heard of. All the same, Pete got a point. You got taken by this young'un and the old man. Hadn't been for Redmile and your woman, you be cooling your butt in the calabozo up at New Hope and we be out our shares."

"To state the matter flat out," Heath said pleasantly, "are you saying we divide the money here and now? Is that it?"

Trask lifted his cold and colorless eyes while his fingers kept shaping the smoke. "That's it."

"Well, I'll tell you, gentlemen. . . ." Heath took a cheroot from his pocket, stuck it in his mouth, and bent over, picking up a thick short branch at the edge of the half-doused fire. He held the glowing end to his cheroot and lighted it. "Pete may indeed have a point. But the sole point which concerns me is where authority resides in this outfit. Doubtless you've heard of me as an arrogant bastard who's accustomed to having his way, and I assure you that you've heard correctly."

Grinning faintly around the cheroot, he squinted against the smoke, meeting Trask's eyes. "In other words, old pot, we divide the money when I damned well say we do and not before then. Clear?"

Pete Ermine heaved forward, his thick trunk swaying, his chin shelving out. "Your goddam say-so don't cut no ice on my pond, mister."

Trask said gently, his eyes on Heath, "Let it ride, Pete. Let it ride."

"Bullshit. Listen, Heath. Me 'n my brothers and Cherokee been trailing together a long time. We come in with you, we taken your orders all right. But we come in for one job at a time. This one's over. We want what's coming to us and you gonna fork it over. That's how it is."

"My, my," Heath murmured. "How it really is—"

Jason would never forget what Heath did next or how he did it. He looked down at the smoldering branch in his fist with a quiet, even disarming smile. Then he took two steps, swinging the heavy chunk of wood back and forward in one savage clubbing motion. Pete Ermine stood flat-footed, his jaw opening, and then flung up an arm to intercept the blow, too late. The chunk took him stiffly across the jaw. His knees folded, his eyes rolled; he pitched forward without a sound. Heath simply stepped aside and let him fall, his outflung arm almost landing in the fire.

Dallas Redmile had moved at almost the same moment. He was edging quietly backward even before Heath took a step. Now he swiftly levered his rifle and said in his mild voice, "Don't nobody twitch a finger."

He was standing slightly behind Trask and Clayt, and

his rifle was pointed loosely at Cherokee, whose hand had dived instinctively to the Bowie knife at his belt. Even the half-breed, alert and cat quick, had been caught flat-footed by the suddenness of it.

"I'm sure nobody will, Dallas," Heath said idly. "Will you, Trask?"

Trask Ermine hadn't stirred a muscle. Eyes still on Heath, he finished shaping his cigarette. "That was taking a pretty long chance, Cap'n. I could of dropped you before the old man got me."

"Part of the game, old pot, living one's chances close to the nerve." Heath laughed softly, his eyes alight and sparking; he tossed the branch away. "I keep my bargains, Trask. We'll split the money when we reach Arrowhead Tanks. That was the agreement to start with. I don't see any reason to change it, do you, now?"

Trask shook his head. He dropped to one knee by his unconscious brother, turned Pete's face out of the dirt, and felt along his jaw. "Leastways you didn't bust it."

Heath raised his brows. "Really? I meant to, you know."

Trask stood up slowly. He flung his cigarette in the fire. "Could be," he said softly, "Pete asked for that. But I want you to know something, Cap'n. No man'd ever do that to me."

"Fine, old pot. And I want you to know something. Next time I have to remind any of you sterling specimens who is top dog of this outfit, the outcome is going to be a lot more permanent. Now let's get moving. We've a good many miles to cover. . . ."

VIII

'**N**ita Cortinas knew the desert country to which she had been bred. She knew about its teeming and tough-fibered creatures and plants; they held no terrors for her. She had lived next to its threats of death and pain all her young life: sudden and fanged death in a rattler's strike; pain that barbed the needles of the *cholla,* which sprang and hooked to a touch, working a throbbing agony into the flesh. But there were gifts of life too, in certain healing herbs and in the watery contents of the *bisnaga* cactus. The difference between living and dying in desert country was a difference between choices; one learned to make the right ones. One learned by mistakes that were painful and toughening. And always there were vistas of fierce beauty from the small to the large, of vast and contemplative silences, that made it all worth the while for one who could see, who could feel.

So 'Nita had found in her sixteen years. She had more than her share of quick and restless curiosity; once or twice it had led her into situations where only luck and native ingenuity had bailed her out. There was the time when, at eleven, she had saddled a mule without telling anyone and had ridden off toward the Santa Catalinas to the north to see if she could find some of the gold of which she'd heard an Anglo prospector tell. Aside from the stage passengers who quickly came and went, a blend of anonymous faces, visitors were rare at Corazon's lonely station. 'Nita had always listened avidly to the talk of these few, and the old gold-hunter's tall tales of riches to be found in the north peaks had fired her young fancies. Thinking of the wealth she might bestow on her family, she had set out for the Catalinas. At first she had been surprised, then uneasy, and finally terrified to find the blue wavering line of the mountains still retreating steadily before her after long hours. Turning back, she'd soon realized she was thoroughly lost. But she'd had the sense to stop where she was, waiting through a long cold night and another long hot day till her father and grandfather had found her. Sun blistered, half-dead of thirst, and thoroughly chastened, she'd afterward come to a deep respect for the desert, but the experience hadn't quelled her curiosity. 'Nita was sure she could cope with anything; it was just a matter of watching and learning.

She'd been encouraged in such pursuits by a leathery maverick of a grandfather who claimed that she reminded him of him—this to the dismay of her parents, who had spoken much of sending her to the home of a distant and wealthy cousin of her father in Mexico City, where she might be schooled to demure and proper ways. A letter requesting the favor had been sent, along with an offer of payment, for a poor Cortinas was no less proud than a rich one. But the cousin's reply, when it had finally come, had been discouraging, which had secretly pleased 'Nita. She was curious about the wide world beyond her small one, but Abuelito's disgusted assurances that all existence there was stiff and stuffy, no better than a prison, had damped any desires in that direction. Here was the freedom of a carefree girlhood with many things remaining to be explored and learned of. To her it was a way of life deeply satisfying, rather than one full of harsh privations, for she had known nothing else.

Now it was done with, wiped out as cleanly as the stroke of an ax might ready a chicken for the pot. The 'dobe-walled station at Corazon was no longer home; it was a place of strangeness and desolation on which she turned her back without regret, except for the sodden lump of grief in her throat.

It did not blunt the keenness of her senses. She rode straight-up and studied with minute care the land she was crossing. 'Nita felt confident, but not foolishly so. She knew her experience as a desert-dweller must be tempered by her ignorance of the desert at large. Not yet six years old when her parents had brought her to Corazon, she'd never traveled over ten miles from it since. She knew that there were other kinds of country at no great distance, that in such places conditions were very different from what she'd always known. The mountain ranges she had seen only from a good way off cradled tall timber and wide grasslands and rushing streams, and there was wild game in abundance and great ranches where *vaqueros* tended herds of white-faced cattle.

Of these things she had often wondered, but she barely thought of them now. Her way was taking her across the powdery white glare of alkali flats and flinty terrain mantled by such scrubby and thorny vegetation as she knew well. This was the way her two gringos had gone, and there she would go. She thought of them that way—her gringos. She had many thoughts, both puzzled and understanding, about the pair. She had a rough comprehension of their mission, though the purposes of each weren't entirely clear. They were very different men, so different that only strong reasons would have brought them so far together on a long trail.

Since 'Nita did not want them to catch sight of her for a while, she rode at an inheld pace, following their sign. This was easy enough in most places, and wherever it was not, she dismounted and had little difficulty studying the sign out. Eventually, of course, she would have to show herself to them, and she guessed they'd be anything but overjoyed. What would they say? It did not matter, she thought stubbornly, except of course that she could say nothing in return, a thought she found quite depressing.

She loosened her headcloth and let the warm wind cool her sweaty throat. Fingering her neck and feeling no pain there, she wondered once more what had happened to her voice. She couldn't recall injuring her throat any more than she remembered hurting her foot. Instinctively she knew that the injury was not physical, that the effort to form words, no matter how hard she tried, was useless.

After riding a long time across sage-covered flats,

she halted to rest her mount. As she unslung her canteen, she heard a distant slam of gunfire. She listened awhile, but there was only the one shot, no more. Uncapping the canteen, she took a small drink, then glanced at the sun. It was lowering, but still hours short of setting. It might be a good idea to overtake the gringos before nightfall.

Pushing on a bit more quickly, she speculated on that single gunshot. Perhaps it meant nothing. A man might fire one shot to bag a quail or jackrabbit. But she was doubly watchful now.

Coming onto the brow of a short rise, she pulled up and shaded her eyes with a hand. There was an oddly shaped ridge somewhat off to her right; a couple of buzzards were wheeling and dipping above it. Something was dead or close to it. Nothing remarkable in that, but the memory of the gunshot gave her a tingle of apprehension.

She gigged her paint swiftly on, hardly bothering to check the horse tracks anymore. They led straight to the ridge; at its base she plainly marked where the two gringos had dismounted. Stepping to the ground, she followed their tracks to where they faded out on the ridge's lower slope. Both horses and men were gone now, but the gringos must have gone up on the ridge for a reason. And there were the buzzards circling insistently above. . . .

She started laboriously up the slope. It was slow going, her sandals in bad shape and flapping loose, her foot catching painful twinges. When she reached the summit, 'Nita saw nothing but a stretch of crumbling rock. She moved carefully across to the far rim and a sharp drop-off. Below was a rolling sage flat; she saw smoke wisping from the site of a recent fire.

Cautiously edging onto the rimrock, she looked straight down. Yards below her, a man's body was hung precariously on a thrust of rock. Though he lay face down on the narrow shelf, grotesquely sprawled, she could tell it was the gray-haired gringo, Penmark.

Dried blood stained his hair and darkened the rock beneath his head. It seemed likely he was dead. If he had fallen from up here, his head must have cracked on the rock. Would his young *compadre* have left him if he were yet alive? Even if he thought the old man was dead, she reasoned, he would not leave the body like this. But what of that shot? Perhaps the men's enemies had shot the old man and had taken the young one prisoner.

Yes, that seemed the answer. The enemies had been camped below, where the fire was, and the two gringos had seen its smoke and had come up here to spy on them. But something had gone wrong; the old man was shot, the young one captured.

'Nita sat down on her heels, studying the almost straight drop below. The cliffside was very rough, and it slanted outward only a little. Could the old one have fallen so far and still be alive? Maybe he had been dead before he fell; they had shot him and thrown his body over. But she could see his hat and rifle at the bottom of the drop. Would they have thrown his rifle down too?

She doubted that she could climb down to him; even if she were able, how would she get his body up? She could think of but one way, and was not at all sure she could manage it. But she must try. If the old man were still alive, if there was the faintest chance he lived, she must try.

'Nita descended the ridge and set to the task of leading her horse up its crumbling flank. She had to fight him all the way, leaning her slight weight against the reins. The final precipitous yards were the worst; the animal balked and shied as rotted rock scaled away under his hooves. When they reached the top, he was lathered and trembling. 'Nita's palms were slick with blood where the reins had cut them.

Taking the coiled reata from her saddle, she secured its noose end around a great block of stone that rested near the rim. She let the other end tumble down the cliff wall; it extended more than a yard past Penmark's body. That was little slack to spare, but it was enough.

Studying the distance to the cliff base, she thought about what would happen if she made a misstep. Then she knew that the best thing was not to think about it. Drying her bloody hands on her skirt, she gripped the rope with all her strength and threw her weight tentatively against it a few times to be sure the noose was secure. The anchoring rock itself was at least six times as heavy as she.

Setting her back to the drop, she slipped gradually over the rim, walking slowly backward and down. The escarpment slanted just enough that her feet could help steady her descent, and for once 'Nita had cause to be glad she was skinny and had wiry muscle in her arms. This was something she could do, she guessed, as well as any boy might do it.

Descending the rope was quite simple, so long as she didn't glance down too often, any more than was necessary to locate footing and to guide her feet onto the ledge. There was less than a foot of space between the wall and Penmark's sprawled form, leaving barely enough room for her to stoop down. She managed to do so, holding the rope with one hand, clasping Penmark's wrist in the other, and moving her fingers till she located a pulse.

It was a good strong pulse. Relief flooded her.

The tricky part now was to let go the rope, freeing both her hands to do what must be done without losing her balance. Penmark's right leg dangled over the abutment, pulling his whole body precariously toward its edge. She'd have to move a little to set the rope; hardly any movement at all would shift his weight slightly toward his overbalanced side. Another inch or so might tip his body over the edge. But the risk must be taken.

'Nita grasped his belt in her right hand and strained with all her strength to raise his body enough to slip the rope end beneath his stomach with her left hand. It was the work of many minutes for her to maneuver the rope to his other side, heaving his belly up a fraction of an inch for a couple seconds at a time, resting briefly between each effort. Meantime she could feel the little telltale jerks as his weight slid outward on the shelf.

Finally she could reach across him and grasp the rope's end. Giving more sporadic tugs on his belt, she hauled several inches of slack into the rope. Enough to enable her to knot it securely around his waist.

That done, there was no danger of his slipping over. 'Nita wiped her palms dry again, then seized hold of the rope and climbed back to the rim. When she stood once more on solid rimrock, a wild quivering seized her; she sat down on the rock, sweating and shaking, till her muscles and nerves steadied.

The paint was reluctant to venture near the rim. It was necessary, however, to urge the fiddlefooting animal close enough for her to slip the noose off the rock and over her saddle horn. Once she'd accomplished this, the rest was comparatively easy. She mounted and reined the paint sideways. He sidled against the rope's taut resistance with the skill of any trained cowpony; Penmark's limp body slowly bumped and rasped up the side of the cliff.

At last the gray-haired gringo lay doubled up on the rimrock. 'Nita removed the rope and then, grasping his wrists, dragged him over to the deep shade of a boulder. Ignoring her own exhaustion, she went over the unconscious man with sensitive hands, trying to determine the extent of his hurts. All his bones seemed to be intact, even his skull. He bore a multitude of bruises and scratches, as well as several great raw abrasions where flesh had scraped away in his fall. Using a strip torn from her skirt and a little canteen water, she soaked away the clotted blood that matted his hair, discovering a straight furrow in his scalp that bared the clean white bone of his skull.

That, she thought, could have been made by a bullet.

She could find no other serious hurts, except the mashed flesh and purpled swelling of his forehead where it must have struck the ledge. It was bleeding a little. He was a tough, strongly muscled old gringo; nevertheless, 'Nita felt a deepening anxiety. A fall such as he had taken could very well jar a man's vitals loose, and there was no telling what had been done to him internally. At least not till he was conscious again, and so far he hadn't twitched an eyelash.

'Nita bathed his face and scalp sparingly. Then she descended the ridge and hunted up a patch of prickly pear. She hacked off several of the flat paddles and, having pared away the spines, carried them back to the ridgetop. After macerating the cactus paddles between a pair of stones she applied the resulting mash to the wounds on Penmark's scalp and forehead. A couple more strips, these torn from her bedraggled petticoat, made bandages to tie the poultices in place.

The sun had tipped low; it flattened to a molten stain along the rim of earth. Wearily the girl spread a blanket over Penmark, then went down the ridge to scour up an armload of brush and carry it up. She built a small fire between sheltering rocks where it wouldn't be seen when darkness came. She carried up several more armfuls of dry wood. Then she cut strips of bacon and laid them in her small skillet. While the bacon was frying, she kneaded cornmeal and salt and a little water together on a flat stone. Cooked in bacon grease, the mixture baked to a crisp gold-brown. She ate half of the bacon and johnny cake and wrapped the rest in an oilcloth.

By now it was full dark and still the gringo had not come to; she wondered if he ever would. She had heard of people staying alive and unconscious for a long time until, for lack of nourishment, they expired. 'Nita shivered as she sat resting her chin on an updrawn knee, studying Penmark's haggard face, its weathered brown gone sallow and bloodless in the firelight. No matter what, she thought with a kind of numb determination, she would not desert this man. If he did not revive, she would stay with him till he died.

She had found *Abuelito's* clasp knife on the ground near his body and picked it up as a sentimental token, but it would be of use for effecting repairs on her disintegrating sandals. It contained a fold-in leather punch as well as big and small blades. She used the tiny awl to poke ravels of cloth through the rope-soles of her sandals, tying them so they would reinforce the fraying straps.

As she worked, she felt her throat lumping painfully with a hundred memories of *Abuelito,* his deft sinewy hands engaged at the leather craft he knew so well. The lump softened like warm wax, and something cold in her stomach seemed to melt; her eyes misted. The tears came at last, crawling down her cheeks, but she couldn't manage to cry aloud, not truly. The sounds she made were more of sodden belchings that rolled up in aching spasms from her throat, hurting clear to the pit of her stomach. She dropped her work, pressing her hands over her mouth and throat, trying to control the ugly sobs that were not sobs.

Penmark groaned quietly. Weakly he moved a hand, lifted it, let it fall to his chest.

'Nita reached with all her will for self-control; she moved on her knees to the gringo's side. She raised his head and rubbed a wet cloth over his face; she rubbed harder. His eyes opened; his cracked lips stirred.

"What is it, girl? Wha? . . ."

She held the canteen to his lips; he rolled the water slowly in his mouth and slowly swallowed.

After a few minutes he essayed to sit up, clasping one hand to his head. His jaw was gritted; beads of sweat stood on his face. 'Nita made one effort to press him back, and he pushed her hand weakly but roughly away. Finally he achieved a sitting position. And then he grabbed at his belly.

"Gawd! . . ." His face was gray and twisted; 'Nita dreaded the worst. But as he steadily rubbed a hand back and forth across his belly, his face relaxed to a tight grimace.

"Feels like I got stomped by a crazy bronc," he muttered. His eyes moved to her face; his brows drew together in an effort at concentration. He looked slowly around him, then back at her. "Fell off that rim . . . all I remember. Christ. How come I ain't busted to hell? How you get me up here?"

She did her best to explain, making careful motions

with her hands. Penmark shook his head impatiently, grimacing again. "Leave it go, girl. . . . I'll puzzle it out later."

He settled his body back on the ground, staring upward. His eyes were clear once more, full of the chill purpose that she remembered. It was a look that might frighten some, but it had never frightened her at all, not even at first.

"Feel like I'm one solid bruise. But don't seem to be nothing broken." His eyes flicked to her for confirmation.

She shook her head, though she didn't really know.

"Good . . . good. I'll make it all right. There's a man I got to find." Again a flicking glance at her. "You come this far. You want to come along?"

'Nita smiled. She was surprised to find that a smile was easy to manage when words were not.

IX

Heath and his people pushed south with no particular haste. Jason judged that this was deliberate on Heath's part: the Ermines were impatient to get to Mexico, and so Heath dawdled. He had quelled one small rebellion, and he meant to keep control of the situation by making no concessions. But he seemed to be riding his luck on a god-awful tight edge. And he seemed to have no better reason for doing it than arrogant pride and the plain hell of it. If the Ermines and Cherokee all turned against his authority at once, it

119

would be four tough hardcases against Heath, old Dallas, and the girl Christy. With his own chance of coming out with a whole skin hanging on the favor of these three, Jason felt anything but comfortable about the odds.

Trask Ermine didn't appear to be cowed by Heath; he simply didn't consider that the question of when to divide the spoils was worth a squabble, much less a shoot-out. And he had the say-so, more or less, with his brothers and the half-breed. In going against Heath, Pete Ermine had also defied Trask's warning, so Pete had got the come-uppance he deserved. That was how Trask seemed to look at it. All the same he was no man to run afoul of, Jason decided glumly. You never knew what someone like Heath might take it in his head to do; he was that kind. If, just for the hell of it, he sat on Trask Ermine too hard, there would be fireworks for sure.

For that matter Jason felt far from secure about his own prospects where Heath was concerned. So far it had suited his whim to yield to Christy's wish, but Jason sensed that this was pretty thin insurance. There was a vital, restless power about Heath that wouldn't shape for very long to any mold, including any to which a woman might attempt fitting him. Christy knew it too. After vehemently arguing that Jason be turned free, she hadn't opposed Heath's decision to take him along as hostage. It must have been her shrewd intent, by asking more than Heath was likely to grant, merely to prevent Jason's throat from being cut on the spot. And it had worked. She knew how to handle Heath. But that sort of female ploy had its limits. The real test of Christy's influence would come once they reached the border, when Heath, no longer needing a hostage, had the choice of turning Jason loose or belatedly cutting his throat.

Jason was grateful to the girl and puzzled by her too. She was something outside of his experience. To Penmark it had been as simple as A and B: there were two kinds of women and she was the wrong kind. Two kinds of women—all the older men Jason had ever heard offer opinion on the subject, including his father, thought the same way. If the years had given any of 'em an inkling it might be otherwise, they weren't admitting it. The lines were firmly drawn in their own heads and wasn't nobody going to tell 'em different.

But Christy was different. Different in a curious, exciting way. It was hard to keep his thoughts, no matter what tack they took, from circling back to her.

Besides, how else did you occupy yourself under the conditions? Jogging along between armed captors across the desert's baking monotony, its heat rolling sullenly against your body, your skin drying and your eyes aching with spotty flickers, all you could do was let your mind drift in weary circuits that got nowhere. Your hands were free to handle your reins, but any break for freedom would be fatal.

Maybe there'd be a chance when they made camp . . . after darkness came. Jason doubted it, but the hapless swing of his thoughts kept hitting a fine edge of desperation. As long as he couldn't be sure of his fate at Heath's hands, it seemed better to watch for any chance that offered itself, whatever the risk.

There was Penmark too. Though he'd had mixed feelings toward the man, Jason felt a sick and genuine regret. If Penmark hadn't been killed outright, he must have been close to death after being shot and falling off the rim, his body snagging up hard. If still alive, he would face a slow and helpless dying, stranded on that naked shelf of rock.

If I get out of this, I will go back there, Jason thought dully. It won't do no good, but I'll go back. His dust-caked lips twitched; it would be exactly the sort of gesture on which Penmark would heap biting ridicule. But Jason had his own way. And that, at least, was one thing that Val Penmark had come to understand. . . .

There wasn't even a remote chance of escape that night, because as soon as they made camp, Jason was tied hand and foot with tough rawhide *peales*. He was briefly unbound so he could eat supper and afterward relieve himself, then tied up again.

Next day, a little before noon, Heath's party reached Arrowhead Tanks.

They were located amid lava beds that ages ago had cooled into contorted swells and spires of bluish-black rock, laced by treacherous chasms and potholes. The tanks took their name from a cluster of natural catch basins where runoff water accumulated. Such basins in desert country were usually unreliable; they might dry up in the summer heat or be reduced to puddles of rancid scum. It was always a matter for concern in a land where travel was circumscribed by the availability and quality of water. The ancient trails worn by animals and nomadic tribes converged on such places or pointedly skirted them. Arrowhead Tanks, despite the harsh and burned-out country that surrounded them, had a reputation for staying wet and drinkable the year around. For that reason, and because antelope and bighorn sheep came to water here, the place had long been a favored camp of Indian bands.

So Heath and his group, picking their way slowly across the lava field, approached the Tanks with their weapons ready. Nearing the cordon of basaltic boulders that surrounded the catch basins, they saw a man tramp out to sight and wave his arm. It was the chunky Mexican Miguel; grinning widely, he motioned them on. They rode into the circle of rocks and dismounted with still and weary movements.

"How are you making it, Miguel?" Heath asked.

"Good, *jefe,* good." The Mexican patted his left arm in its dirty sling. "The arm, she's hurt like hell, but the fever, she's wear out. *Dios,* is good to see you! I'm think maybe we see each other in hell next."

Heath chuckled. "A premature thought, I'm glad to say."

He gave orders for setting up camp. The packs were dumped in a sandy clearing between the huge-slabbed boulders. The horses, including Jason's and Penmark's, were led to drink and then picketed on some bear grass that grew sparsely among the rocks. Jason was trussed up again and left in a patch of rock-flung shade. He sat glowering at the outlaws, nursing a mighty thirst along with his bitter worry, but damned if he was going to ask 'em for anything.

Trask Ermine stood hip-shot, right arm dangling along his gun butt; lefthanded, he smoked a cigarette, bringing it to and away from his lips in a kind of deliberate rhythm. He was watching Heath.

Pete Ermine sidled up to Trask at his thick rolling gait. The whole side of Pete's face was swollen purple where Heath had walloped him. His eyes were bloodshot with pain and lack of sleep; he could hardly manage to talk. He mumbled something in his brother's ear. Trask shook his head, giving a brief irritable reply.

Jason wondered if things would break wide open here and now. They were all conscious of the tension, both factions casually wary of one another, but not ready to push it unless the leaders gave a signal. Heath was talking quietly with Dallas, who was watching Trask and Pete. Cherokee and Clayt Ermine stood off to one side, Miguel quietly keeping an eye on them both. Christy was on her knees building a fire; she was tired, her eyes dark circled, but alert to all that was going on.

"Cap'n," said Trask.

Heath ignored him and he repeated it; Heath gave him a careless nod. "What is it, old man?"

"Time for a divvy, I reckon. You said Arrowhead Tanks. We're here."

124

"Ah yes. . . ." Heath touched his mustaches. "Well, now we're here, no rush, eh? We'll make the split before we leave."

"How long you mean to lay over?"

"We can all use a spot of rest. A day. Perhaps two days."

"This don't seem a likely time for it. We're close to the border. Can raise it before nightfall if we hustle."

Heath lifted an eyebrow. "Yes, old pot, but the horses are about done in. Wouldn't want to ride 'em to death, would you? Bit of rest will do wonders for 'em, don't you agree?"

Trask flicked his cigarette butt to the ground. "I tell you, Cap'n. I got a place between my shoulders itches like hell. Only thing's going to scratch it is getting clean across that line. Maybe we thrown off pursuit, maybe not. But you said it yourself. There's law down this way too. It might of got word on us. Could be the damnfoolest thing you ever done, holding us here without need."

Heath was standing side-on to the brothers; he swung on his heel to face them. "Apparently, old pot, the details of our arrangement haven't quite penetrated your skull. Let me clarify them. Once we are across the border, you are free to follow your fancies wither they take flight. Until then, you are under my command."

"Is that right."

"That's right, laddie, and if you're curious as to what I'd do should you chaps take it in your heads to pack up and clear out now . . . why, nothing. Absolutely nothing." Heath slightly spread his hands, smiling. "Of course you'll leave here without your shares. A broken agreement is no agreement, as I see it."

His eyes were wickedly alight and sparking again. He was tough-cored and fearless; he liked the play of power and of matching his wits against an established order of things. But at the heart of it all was a reckless willingness to throw everything on a single cast of the dice, a momentary turn of the cards. That was the real meat and drink of living for Heath. And it was the no-man's territory where Trask Ermine, just as fearless, just as tough in his way, did not tread. These two men understood each other, and Jason vaguely understood that this was why a real confrontation, a testing of mettle, might be inevitable between them. For under-standing or not, there was always that hair-breadth margin of doubt where each man, one boldly, the other cautiously, couldn't help asking himself: *What will he do—if?*

Trask didn't rise to the bait. His scarred face twitched; he said "Shit!" in a flat, positive voice. Turning on his heel, he walked stiffly over to Clayt and Cherokee, saying something to them in a low, angry tone. Pete stared red-eyed at Heath for a long moment, then moved over by his brothers.

There'd be no showdown—at least not yet. . . .

Christy prepared a meal of bacon and tomatoes and pan bread. Jason watched her covertly; she was free striding, her movements quick, firm, and bouncy. Even in a man's shirt, a shapeless calf-length skirt, and tall

126

moccasins, her body curved like a milkmaid's. Her features were clean angled and striking, too sharp for mere prettiness; her hair was cropped boyishly close to her head shaping it like a smooth coppery helmet. She had a wide soft-looking mouth and the boldest eyes Jason had ever seen; they shone softly or hardened like green flints, no in-between.

The men ate in silence, bleakly watchful of each other. They ignored Jason, and he, stretched out in the shade, tried to ignore his thirst and hunger. When they'd finished eating, Christy said, "How about feeding the boy, Jack?"

Heath nodded. "Untie him, Cherokee. And watch him."

The half-breed loosened Jason's hands and stood by while Christy brought him a plate of food and a cup of coffee. As she set them beside him, she leaned close and whispered, "You keep looking so hard, Buster, you'll get sunstruck."

Bending his hot face above his plate, Jason ate hungrily.

When he'd finished, Cherokee escorted him a short ways from the camp so he could tend his needs. The half-breed wore a gun but disdained to draw it; Jason had the feeling his real weapon was the knife at his belt, its beaded sheath cocked at a ready angle. His dark, contemptuous stare said plain as words that he wouldn't mind a reason to use it. Jason was careful not to give him one. Cherokee was compact and hard knit, with muscles like wire rope.

Jason was permitted to wash up at one of the pools; when they returned to camp, Cherokee tied his hands in front of him, not in back, and left his feet unbound. With their bellies full and the midday heat working into them, the men gradually relaxed their bitter vigilance. Cherokee and Miguel and Pete Ermine stretched out for siestas; Heath and Dallas idly conversed; Clayt Ermine dug out a bottle of whiskey and a greasy deck of cards and cajoled Trask into a game. Christy gathered up the dirty utensils and carried them to a pool for washing; she winked at Jason as she passed him, strutting her hip movements more freely than usual.

Clayt took a long pull at the bottle, following her with his eyes. Trask jogged him back to the game with an irritable word. Clayt had no belly for liquor; he became flushed and talkative and finally, when Trask told him to shut up, lapsed into a surly silence. Then he broke out again, accusing his brother of belly stripping; with a disgusted curse, Trask threw down his cards, got up, and walked away.

The afternoon wore drowsily on. Pretty soon everyone but Dallas and Christy was napping in the shade. The girl sauntered over to Jason and halted by him, resting a hand on her hip as she sipped a cup of water. Her green eyes were amused and teasing.

"Want a drink, Buster?"

He nodded. She bent a little to hand him the cup, her breasts stirring gently forward; they formed two firm springy cones against the man's shirt. Face burning, he held the cup awkwardly between his hands and drank, taking a wrong-way swallow that made him cough, spilling the water. Christy took the cup from him, laughing quietly.

Dallas was sitting cross-legged against a rock, mending his bridle. He grunted and stretched his legs, saying mildly, dryly, "Missy, you do like to play hell, don't you?"

She yawned, making a face at him. "You know a better way to pass time?"

"Well, you looking to keep that boy alive, you best watch your fooferawing. Jack's got a jealous eyes."

She walked over to Dallas, lifted his hat, and playfully ruffled his gray hair. "You're the jealous one, you old booger. Admit it."

Chuckling, Dallas grabbed back his hat, giving her a slap on the flank. "Go on, quit your deviling. Go take a bath or something."

"That's a grand idea. Want to join me?"

"Honey, was I twenty years younger, you wouldn't offer."

"You was twenty years younger, old booger, I wouldn't have to."

"That's a thought."

Christy laughed. She got her sack of possibles and dug out a towel and a piece of soap, then headed for one of the rock-sheltered pools.

Jason curled up on his side, bound hands tucked against his chest. He pretended to sleep, but he was fiercely alert, his heart pounding. With his movements hidden from Dallas, he began to work his hands slowly

129

back and forth, twisting against the rawhide strands. The spilled water had drenched his wrists, soaking the dry and flinty *peales*. They were slick and greasy now, and he could feel them gradually, almost imperceptibly, start to stretch with his efforts.

Meantime his head was tipped so he kept Dallas just inside his line of sight, watching him from slitted eyes. The old outlaw was yawning as the sun worked into him, making him drowsy. Finally his hands grew still, his chin sank to his chest.

Jason fought his bonds with a silent fury now, using his teeth as well. His wrists were rasped raw, the skin broken and bleeding, before he finally jerked a hand free of the loops.

Lying motionless, he studied the sleeping outlaws. He needed a horse. Try to sneak one away, he was bound to rouse them. Could maybe get his hands on one of their guns and get the drop, but there were seven to face, seven tough and violent men. If just one tried to fight the drop, so would the rest; most he could hope was to take out one, maybe two, before they got him.

His only chance was with a hostage. One he could handle.

Edging noiselessly to his feet, Jason slipped across the camp and into the boulder-flanked aisle where he had seen Christy disappear. Bending low, he crept between the looming basalt slabs into a brush-grown gully. He heard a faint splashing of water; then it ceased. He paused, listening, then worked upward from the gully toward a corner of angled rock. Beyond it he caught a glint of water at the pool's rim.

Jason came quickly around the rock. Christy was sitting on the edge of the pool, wet hair clinging to her head; she had donned her shirt and skirt and was pulling on one of her long moccasins. She looked up, her eyes rounding. Jason had eyes only for the jacket on the ground beside her, thinking of the little gun she carried in one of its pockets.

He took a long stride forward and dived for the jacket. Landing on his belly with a grunt, he made a wild grab at it. At the same moment Christy snatched it up and rolled away, tearing the jacket from his grasp, then scrambling to her feet. Jason made another wild grab, this time at one of her ankles, but his fingers skidded on her damp skin; she spun away, quick as an eel.

She plunged a hand into the jacket, trying to find the gun in its tangled folds. Jason floundered to his feet as she gave a ripe oath, then tried to dart past him to the gully. His arms flung around her and whirled her off her feet.

She let out a screech, writhing and kicking, and the two of them tumbled to the ground. It took Jason several precious, struggling moments to subdue the girl, pinning her wrists with one hand, trying to push her face in the sand to muffle her cries and unpry her fingers from the jacket, all at the same time.

As he got the jacket away from her, he heard a crunch of running feet in the gully. Frantically he tried to shake loose the pistol, whose weight he could feel in the jacket's folds.

Then Cherokee came pounding around the angled rock. He was on them in a moment, his foot sweeping up. The hard, curled toe of his moccasin slammed Jason in the face and knocked him over backward.

He crawled to his hands and knees, dimly aware of the men pulling around him, a jumble of voices. Then a boot drove into his ribs. The knifelike pain of the kick was lost in a rain of other blows, booted feet smashing at him from all sides. Dark light exploded in his head; he felt nothing more.

X

Penmark spent a bad night, and so did 'Nita Cortinas, kept awake by his groanings and mutterings. Neither of them got much sleep. When a sickly daylight crawled across the sky ahead of the sun, the gringo was on his feet—swaying dizzily, hardly able to stand, but standing.

His body, 'Nita knew, was pummeled to a mass of bruises; his shirt was stiffened by patches of dried blood from many cuts. His face was pasty except for a dull burn of fever in his gaunt cheeks. His eyes were glassy with fever. He kept holding his stomach, which, she guessed, had taken most of the impact of the fall. If anything was broken inside, he would probably be unable to stand; but with this gringo, it was hard to be sure.

He was iron tough and full of a grinding purpose such as she had never seen. And, she realized, perhaps he was a little mad. Thinking of this, she felt for the first time a small lance of fear.

"All right, girl," he said hoarsely. "Let's be packing. Get the stuff together. . . ." His brows puckered in sweating concentration. "Had a rifle, a good Sharps rifle. It must of . . ."

He hobbled over to the rimrock and peered downward, so heedlessly near its edge that a noiseless cry welled in her throat. "It's there. You get the stuff readied, meet me below."

Moving slowly, as if each step was agony, he clambered across the ridgetop and began to descend. Quickly 'Nita saddled and bridled the paint horse and crammed the saddlebags and blanket roll with her slender gear and provisions. She coaxed the paint into a painstaking descent of the ridge, then led him around to its other side. Penmark was sitting on a rock, examining the rifle.

"It's all right," he muttered. "It'll do." He picked up his crumpled hat and beat it into shape, then set it on his bandaged head. Then he stood up, swayed for balance, and stumbled over to the paint horse. Grasping the saddle leather, he looked at her glazedly and said, "There's just the one horse. We ride him by turns, eh? That all right with you?"

She nodded.

"Jesus, I'm dizzy . . . hold him steady."

'Nita gripped the rein close to the bit, anxiously watching Penmark toe into the stirrup. He set his weight and heaved himself upward, pitched astride with an agonized grunt, swayed over, then caught his balance. He straightened in the saddle, holding to the pommel one-handed, his eyes stark as slate.

"How you on track?"

She wanted to cry at him that this was no good, he was too sick, knowing that if she could shape the words, they'd be futile. She gave a small nod.

"Then you follow it. From there, see where that fire was? All right, get moving now. Lead out."

Walking slowly, 'Nita led the paint horse across the sage flat toward the broken country beyond. The people they were following had many horses; the trampled sign was so clear she did not even think about it. She didn't see how they'd ever overtake the people at such a pace as this. But if the sick gringo would not have it otherwise, she must follow the trail until . . . until he could continue no farther.

Maybe he would not be willing to stop till he was dead. But what could she do?

She looked back at him often and anxiously. He held to the pommel with one hand, the other gripping his rifle as if frozen around it. He swayed and rolled dangerously, his chin bouncing on his chest. How long could he keep it up? *El viejo,* she thought wryly. With such a *viejo,* there was no telling.

The immediate country changed as she moved on, but 'Nita easily held her general bearings. At her back were the bald heights of the Santa Catalinas; southward rose the purple sawtooths of the Santa Ritas, while south and east the San Ignacio range bent into

Mexico. She thought that, given time, she could find her way to any place whose general location she knew, even if she hadn't been there. Towns and camps were widely scattered in the region, but many were linked by roads that she could follow. Either the gringo would drive himself to death or he would become too sick and helpless to resist her, and then she would look for a town. And help for the gringo, if he still lived. . . .

As there was no question of taking turns with the horse, she must walk for as long as she could keep going. Her big worry was water. They had a single small canteen of it to divide between them; she was determined to manage without water herself as long as possible. Several times she made a halt to give Penmark a drink; pretending to drink from the canteen, she barely moistened her lips.

Noon came and went. By then Penmark was in a terrible way. She didn't know what was holding him in the saddle. His color was ghastly, his fever climbing. Yet he refused even to pause for a rest, perhaps knowing that if he left the saddle, he wouldn't make it back up. She knew from his mumblings that he had lost all sense of time; he spoke of sunset being an hour away, though it was early afternoon. She guessed that the end of his endurance was close.

It came suddenly. One moment he was riding head up, briefly and relentlessly erect. The next, he was canting sideways, pitching heavily to the ground. He fell face down and then, groaning, struggled to push himself up. He managed only to roll onto his back.

"Help me, girl . . . get me up again . . . tie me on."

'Nita shook her head.

"Goddam . . . your . . . bead-counting heathen soul."

His eyes closed; he didn't move again. She knelt by him and shook him gently. Then laid her ear to his chest. He was alive and unconscious, and hopefully would stay that way a good while.

They had stopped in a vast rock field, a raw and broken sweep of splintered red boulders and slablike monoliths. Seizing hold of Penmark's arms, she tugged him into the shadow of a boulder. It was a few minutes' work to hobble the horse and to make the man as comfortable as she could, digging a hollow in the sand for his hips and covering him with a blanket. 'Nita gave the canteen a shake, finding the water nearly gone. Taking stock of her dwindling provisions too, she knew she must find a way of stretching them for two people. That she could manage, but water was the real concern.

She set out to explore the area, working outward in a slow circle. The vegetation was scanty, but she found enough to serve her purpose: squaw cabbage and puffballs, mesquite beans and juniper berries. Continuing on, she stopped often to rest and to rub her aching legs. Oddly, a half-day's grueling hike had worked out her limp. It was almost gone, but her feet wouldn't last through another trek like today's. They were lacerated by rock and thorn, raw with pain that shot into her calves at every step. The pebbly, baking soil felt like a red-hot plate on her soles. Her sandals were nearly finished, beyond repair.

She came to a shallow dry wash laced with brush that was full of quail runways. It was a good find, but she came on a better one a little way down the wash. Scraping noises attracted her to a low spot where a couple of porcupines were busily digging. The animals waddled off at her approach. 'Nita dropped to her knees by the hole they'd made and clawed out more earth to deepen it. When her fingers touched moist sand, she worked feverishly to widen the bottom till a broad cup was formed.

She sat back on her heels, watching water seep up in a cloudy puddle. It would take time for the hole to fill and the water to clear, but she knew with a surge of relief that the most pressing need was solved. . . .

Before the day was over, 'Nita had snared two quail in running nooses she'd set in the runways; these she spitted on a stick and slow-roasted over a good bed of coals. She sliced up a puffball and fried the pieces in bacon grease; along with roasted root of squaw cabbage, it would stretch out to several good meals. She'd cooked up mesquite beans to make a palatable coffee. The paint horse was well fed on mesquite beans and juniper berries, his thirst satisfied.

She mashed up more prickly pear and changed the poultices on Penmark's head. His fever peaked swiftly; he thrashed about and raved disjointedly. 'Nita built the fire to a roaring blaze and kept him covered with blankets to help sweat out the fever. She got him to take a little water. Finally he quieted down; he slept.

By then it was sunset, and she was too exhausted to do anything but sit by the fire and stare dully at the flames. From the gringo's delirious talk, she could put together in a rough way the story of his wife's death and the reason of his bitter mission.

She rested her crossed arms on her updrawn knees, gazing at the sleeping man's face—a harsh and craggy face even in repose. What would he do when he came to his senses? She dreaded the worst, for even drained by fever, he might be more than she could handle. He would get well only if he stayed quiet; even great weakness, she feared, would not abate the iron fury in the man.

'Nita's face sank gradually onto her arms. It would do no harm to sleep, but she did not want to sleep too soundly; she must wake quickly if he needed her.

She woke with a start. It was full dark, and she knew that she had slept for hours. The night chill had crept into her flesh; the fire had died to a handful of cherried embers. She rubbed her arms, shivering, and then built up the fire. The wash of light glanced on Penmark's face, and she saw it was turned toward her. His eyes were open, half-lidded but clear.

" 'Lo, sis," he whispered.

Her throat worked convulsively. *¡Santa Maria!* If only she could get out the words she wanted to. Tell him he must be still and not excite himself. Maybe it would do no good, but what a thing it would be to say the words.

"Reckon . . . I damn near killed myself . . . and you.

138

Damnfool thing to do. Must of been way out of my head. Well . . ." His eyes tipped away from her face. "I want to last awhile yet. I got to last. Jesus, I got me a thirst. Could drink a river dry."

She wasn't slow in making him understand they had plenty of water; she showed him the food she had improvised. And then she found him looking at her strangely, as though he were seeing her for the first time.

"Been busy as a bee in clover, ain't you?" His lips barely stirred, but she had the startled thought that he wasn't far from a smile. "Well, that's fine. You been plenty lucky for me. We're going to make it all right, sis. We're going to make it out together."

Penmark didn't rouse next day until nearly noon. He had slept like a log; he moved stiffly and slowly, but his dizziness had abated with the fever. According to him, he'd gotten as much rest as he needed; it was time to move along. When the paint was readied, he mounted and swung 'Nita up behind him. And they took up the two-day-old trail.

They made better time now, but as the day waned, so did the paint's stamina. 'Nita's hundred pounds and Penmark's two hundred, plus saddle and gear, added to a stiff burden. Penmark chafed with impatience, but was cold-headed enough to hold the paint to a reasonable pace. Still, the heat and the weight were wearing the animal down.

In the late afternoon, they halted on the summit of a

rise thinly forested with mesquite that stood almost head-high to a man. Penmark grunted, "Rest," and they dismounted. Wincing a little, he hobbled to the edge of the ridge and hunkered down, studying the land south and west. 'Nita broke out some cold grub and sat down on the warm sand beside him, setting the food between them. He ate slowly, not looking at her. She watched him covertly, thinking he was like a gaunt gray lobo, a grim wolf of a man empty of everything but his driving purpose. Under control now, it still seethed in him like cold acid.

"Losing time to beat hell," he muttered around a mouthful of food, "but no help for it. Horse'll founder, we keep this up. We better walk a spell." His eyes turned coldly on her. 'Nita lowered her gaze self-consciously, rubbing a long scratch on her bare leg. "Hell," he said abruptly, "you can't walk on them feet. You ride."

He washed down a last mouthful of food with a drink from the canteen, then started to get up. Swiftly then, he pulled back down, closing a hand around 'Nita's wrist to hold her beside him. She followed the direction of his stare toward a crumbling height some distance off right of them. For a moment she couldn't discern what had caught his attention.

Then she fixed on a flicker of dull color. This resolved itself into a pair of riders. They were picking their way down the rocky, angular face of the height.

"We'll keep down," Penmark murmured. "Wait."

She felt a touch of apprehension as he fingered his

rifle. They waited for endless minutes, watching the horsemen move off the high scarp and onto the desert floor. They were heading generally this way; their line of advance should bring them within a few hundred feet of the mesquite-covered ridge.

As they came clearly into sight, 'Nita felt the slow, crawling terror of recognition. These were Apaches. She could see their breechcloths and long leggin-moc-casins and the red kerchiefs tied around their heads. Even under a bright blaze of sun, fear stabbed her flesh like icy quills; her tongue went thick and dry and seemed to fill her mouth. The screams of her murdered family echoed in her head.

"Hostiles," Penmark said quietly. "Tell you what I'm going to do, little girl. I'm going to get us a horse. Maybe a couple of horses. You sit tight now. . . ."

He brought the rifle to his shoulder and set his eyes along the sights. But he didn't fire. He waited through another endless drag of time while the two Apaches slowly angled this way. They were in no hurry. In addition to their mounts, they had a packhorse with the carcass of a bighorn sheep tied across it.

'Nita's mind was numb to everything but a chill clarity of physical detail. She felt a hot wind press across the ridge and saw it skirl up dust along the flats beyond; she saw the men's dark-copper skins and the bright warpaint that barred their faces. She knew a sickness of cold panic held in leash only by the paralysis that gripped her limbs.

The drumroll of her pulse filled her ears like thunder.

141

If she were not voiceless, if a scream could have forced itself from her swollen throat, she would have screamed.

Penmark's rifle shifted almost imperceptibly to the men's approach. They were crossing directly in front of the ridge's south flank. If they had any intimation of danger, they gave no sign of it.

The rifle made its sullen boom.

As if a trigger had been touched in her too, 'Nita fell on her hands and knees; her mouth opened wide to scream. But if she made any sound, it was lost in the waves of gunroar that crashed and beat in her ears. She saw the buckskin horse in the lead fold down as if pole-axed, and his rider pitch forward over his head.

The other Apache reined up, throwing a wild glance around. Penmark was already ramming another shell into his breech; this time he took only a fleeting instant to pull his bead.

The shot wiped the second brave from horseback as if he'd been struck by an unseen fist. He hit the ground like a bundle of brown rags and lay unmoving.

The first man had lit on all fours and had promptly scrambled to his feet. He paused only momentarily as he saw his companion hit the dust; then he made a wild leap for the second Apache's horse. He caught its rein and swung astride. Whirling the animal around, he kicked it into a run toward the west, bending low to its neck and drumming his heels. He was racing for a deep gulch whose banks were flanked by heavy mesquite and catclaw.

Cursing savagely, Penmark breeched another shell and settled his sights. He pulled trigger. 'Nita saw the bullet kick up dust in front of the running horse. The Apache slowed as he reached the steep-sided gulch, then plunged his mount into it. He cut swiftly away along its bottom, half-concealed by the banks; only fleeting glimpses of him showed above its brush-laced rim.

Penmark fired twice more. Then the Apache was lost to sight where the gulch curved into a jumble of sandstone rises; he was gone.

"Goddam it!" The oath slashed from Penmark's lips like a knife; he straightened up, swiping a fist across his sweating face. "Got clean away. . . . If he makes smoke, we got trouble."

He started down the rise at a stiff trot. 'Nita crawled to her feet; her trembling legs threatened to give way. Stumbling painfully over the rough ground, she followed him.

Penmark's bullet had creased the buckskin horse at the exact point where his neck swelled into his withers. Momentarily stunned, he was thrashing his legs now, struggling to regain his feet. Penmark ran to him and seized the trailing horsehair halter that was the Apache's only rein. The buckskin lunged upright and reared, and Penmark hauled him down with an iron hand.

"Whoa there . . . whoa!"

Gradually the horse calmed, tremors rippling over his glossy coat. Another rope trailed from the buckskin's neck to the halter of the packhorse, a solid and short-coupled bay. Unable to bolt, this animal had stayed quiet, shuffling a little, his ears laid back.

Penmark was talking to both animals, soothing horse-talk, as 'Nita came up. She halted a few yards away, her arms limp at her sides. She looked at the sprawled body of the Apache, twisted half on its side; her throat worked silently. Then she saw the man's arm move—only his arm, inching stealthily around to his hip where a knife was sheathed. Penmark's back was to him.

'Nita opened her mouth to cry at Penmark. Nothing.

The Apache's quartz-tipped lance lay about two yards from her feet, flung there when the bullet had driven him backward. She bent and snatched it up. In the same instant the Apache pulled his knife and rolled slowly and painfully onto his rump. She saw the ripple of long cordy muscles under his skin, which glistened with blood and sweat; and the dark-copper face, fiercely barred with blue and vermilion, squeezed into a savage grimace.

He got one knee under him and lurched to his feet.

'Nita ran forward. A cry burst from her lips. She held the lance in a two-handed grip, straight out before her and thrust blindly and without conscious volition. She saw the Apache's eyes focus on her in that last second. And then he toppled back like a falling tree, the lance sticking up from the arch of his belly where it met his barrel chest.

He twitched and groaned, chopping his knife into the

144

earth. Then his fist balled hard around the hilt and he was still. . . .

'Nita stood as she was, gazing at the dead man, till she felt Penmark's hands on her shoulders. He started to say something, and she turned blindly against him, her cheek pressed to his chest, her fingers closing and opening and closing again on his arms. Her body shook with a wild, convulsive sobbing.

Penmark didn't say anything for a time. When he did, he wasn't so much speaking to her as spelling his thoughts aloud. "Them two was out hunting . . . main band can't be far away. Cayetano's crowd, I reckon, and they are swinging back south. And," he added grimly, "we killed one and let one get away. That'll fix us 'less we make tracks."

Moving 'Nita aside, he tramped over to the Apache, kneeled down, and peeled off the dead man's tall moccasins. He walked back to the girl, holding the moccasins out. "Here. Pull these on. Don't lose no time about it. We—"

"No!" She shrank back a step, her eyes fixed on the moccasins. "No!"

Penmark was silent for a surprised moment; flesh crinkled quizzically at the corners of his eyes. "So. Found your voice at last, huh? You understand me all right?"

"*Sí* . . . yes." Her voice was a strained whisper.

"Then you get them things on. We got no time to waste."

Her lips thinned; she shook her head.

145

Penmark's voice deepened harshly. "Sister, I ain't going to tell you again. Put 'em on. Or I'll put 'em on you, if I have to bust both your legs to do it. *¿Comprende?*"

She reached out a hand and touched the stiff leather, shuddering. Then she took the moccasins from him and sat down to tug them on.

XI

The sky at dawn was a strange color. Jason had never seen anything like it: a grimy yellow overcast that filled it from horizon to horizon. The sun had a weak and hazy glow, as if its strength had been dissipated into the brassy stain that overlay the sky and land. The men roused sluggishly from their blankets, looking owlish and tired. The half-breed Cherokee was restless and uneasy; he prowled around and outside of the camp, muttering to himself.

Trask Ermine spoke to him, then approached Heath. "Cap'n, he says there's a storm coming. A bad one. High wind and a lot o' sand."

"Sandstorm, eh? I've heard of 'em."

"I been in one," Ermine said curtly. "Like to tear all hell loose when they hit. It's coming fast and we're in a bad place for it. Could of been out of its way, maybe, we'd kept moving yesterday. Now all we can do is lay low and wait it out."

They did everything that could be done in the way of preparing for it. The horses were herded into the deep cover of an arroyo; the canteens were filled. A rude tent of blankets was arranged in a pocket among the bulges of lava, and they lugged their belongings under its shelter.

Huddled on his side, Jason watched their preparations. He was so sore from the savage beating they'd fetched him yesterday that he doubted he could move a muscle even if he hadn't been tied hand and foot. Raging at his attempt to escape, the men had worked him over with fists and boots till he'd lost consciousness. Since that time they had simply ignored him; nobody had offered him water or food last night or this morning. His mouth was a furry kiln, his head buzzing; it was hard to fix his thoughts on anything. Stabs of pain in his sides made him numbly wonder if some of his ribs were busted; sick as he felt, he almost didn't give a damn.

A brooding silence had settled on the desert. There was no stir of wind, no movement of any kind. No lizard scuttled; no bird flew. Even the occasional calls of quail from brush and stunted trees had died away in the vast quiet. Over everything lay a pall of yellowish heat that throbbed all around, making you feel like a scorched ant trapped at the bottom of a limitless bowl.

Far off and faintly, Jason caught a dim roar of sound. He had no idea where it was coming from, nor could he make out any change in the sickly sky. Yet the noise was steadily swelling in volume; he fancied he could feel it vibrating through the hot earth. And then he knew a first icy crawl of panic. As a boy, he had huddled in a

147

root cellar on the edge of a tornado; he remembered clinging to his mother, and he remembered how the awesome roar of wind had shattered all your perspectives and your judgments, causing the whole world to shrink to a few square feet of terrifying darkness.

And he sensed how this might be worse, a hundred times worse, and why they were likely in the worst possible place to encounter it. Vast dunes of naked sand lay to the east and south, and some to the north as well. Thinking of the destruction wrought by that long-ago tornado, how it had uprooted great trees and hurled building timbers about like baby's toys, he had an inkling of what a powerful wind would do to tons upon tons of loose sand.

Did the others intend to leave him out in the middle of it? Something akin to pure horror seized Jason; he kicked feebly with his legs, trying to croak out a yell from his parched throat.

Christy was heading for the shelter, a pair of bulging saddlebags slung from her shoulder. She halted and gave him a long look. Since his rough manhandling of her, she'd ignored him as completely as had the others; he felt a sinking conviction that she was in no mood to do him more favors. Whatever her mood was, though, she dropped the saddlebags and came over, knelt by him and cut away his leg ropes. Then she helped him to his feet. Leaning heavily on her, hardly able to move one foot ahead of the other, Jason stumbled to the hollow between the lava slabs, dropped to his knees, and rolled into it under the blankets.

Nobody said anything. They were all occupied with shoving saddles and other plunder into the space. One by one now, they crawled under the blankets and sandwiched themselves side by side with their backs to the rocks.

Even in this jammed closeness, pressed in a corner with Cherokee crouched sweatily beside him, Jason was aware that the pulsing quilt of heat had loosened, drawing up from the ground as if pulled by invisible strings. All of nature seemed to pause in a lull of sullen suspense, and still the thunder of approaching wind grew constantly. He felt static charges prickle the hair at the back of his neck.

Now the patch of sky he could see through a gap in the blankets was hazing from yellow to tan, the weird glow fading, darkening under a turgid front of sand particles that towered thousands of feet high. Not a mile away, it was rushing toward the lava beds. Out on the flats, tumbleweeds bounced like jackrabbits, riding the first sweep of wind—an icy wind that flicked under the shelter in gusty whips, chilling to the bone with a swift fury that was startling, frightening, in the wake of that furnace heat.

They grasped hold of the blankets and clutched them tight. The pocketing hollow was partly exposed to the blast of wind-borne sand as it struck; it took their combined strengths to hold down the flapping soogans in those first wild moments. Then the fierce torrent of wind and sand became a howling pressure that built up against the flimsy barrier, and their efforts were turned

149

to forcing a space around their heads. The wind blew colder and colder. Its thunderous din increased till all their senses were drowned in a blind maelstrom where time and space meant nothing, where body and mind became suspended in a nightmare cocoon somewhere between solid earth and boiling sky.

That was the worst of it for Jason—not the pounding violence of wind and sand, not the marrow-eating cold, not the gritty tempest of sand that beat through the mesh of thick-weave blankets, scouring his nose and throat, searing like sandpaper between his tight-shut eyelids. No, it was the loss of all direction, of near and far, of high and low—of everything but the seething malevolence of nature gone out of control, righting some timeless imbalance in its mysterious chemistry with one screaming drawn-out surge.

So the storm wore on, for a numbing and measureless space of minutes into hours. Finally its savage eternity was spent; it died away. But long before that happened, their flesh and nerves had been battered beyond feeling and beyond caring. . . .

When they began to stir at last, it was with the frayed and uncertain motions of drugged people. Sand had mounded against the blankets, half-burying them; it cascaded away from their bodies as they pushed free. Christy straightened up cautiously, easing the cramps from her legs, her arms. A tinny ringing filled her ears; her mouth and eyes were sore as the devil. Her skin felt gritty all over, and her only thought at the moment was of washing up.

"Well, what about it now?" Trask Ermine said harshly. "Do we ride or not?"

"We ride." Heath stretched his arms, yawning. "Let's get our plunder together, folks. Cherokee, have a look at the horses. See how they weathered it out."

The half-breed tramped away toward the arroyo. Christy tried shaking the sand from her clothing, then gave it up. "Lordy, Jack, I need a bath."

Heath gave her a faintly amused look. "Well, make it quick, angel. That's if you've a taste for another sand scrubbing."

"What?"

"Go see for yourself."

She slogged through the loose, ankle-deep sand to one of the lava basins. She halted and stared, then eyed Heath with a cool disgust. "It's half-full of sand. And dry as a bone, no less."

"Naturally it is, my dear. Sand particles in a storm like that one are so charged and dry, they literally draw up moisture like a sponge."

"Got that out of some fancy-ass book, didn't you?"

Heath laughed.

Christy was in no mood for what he considered humorous. She went back to the hollow where they had taken refuge, dug her saddle free of the sand, and shook her soogans out. Jason Drum was sitting against a nearby rock, dust caked and dazed. Christy regarded his bruised face without much sympathy;

151

she was still sore from his roughing her up. Then she noticed his hands, the fingers discolored and swollen like sausages from the brutally tight ropes on his wrists, and had to steel herself against pity. He had it coming, she thought. She'd been sure of persuading Jack to set him free at the border. Now, she was far from certain. . . .

Cherokee came up from the arroyo, leading two horses. As always his dark face was unreadable, but Christy thought he looked glummer than usual. He halted, looking at Pete and Clayt Ermine as he spoke.

"Horses all gone. All but these."

"Gone?" Heath paused in the act of lighting a cheroot. "What do you mean, gone?"

"They pull pickets, drift away with storm. These two deep in rocks, they stay. All others gone."

Everyone looked at the two Ermines now, and Miguel murmured, *"¡Jesus Maria!"*

"Pulled their pickets," Heath echoed. "You two had charge of . . . for the love of God, didn't you put proper hobbles on the beasts?"

Pete Ermine's jowls had whitened under his whisker stubble; he cleared his throat. "Well, Christ," he muttered, "we ground-tied 'em good, and they was sheltered good in them banks, that should of . . ."

"You . . . stupid . . . bastards." Trask Ermine spoke with an ominous quiet, staring at his brothers. "Something that simple, you can't do it right. Too damn simple for you jugheads!"

Heath gazed at the tip of his cheroot. "Well, gen-

152

tlemen. You've landed us in a pretty fix. What do you think happens now?"

At once Trasks's anger veered; his stare pounced at Heath. "Way I reckon, that ain't for you to say. Much your doing as anyone's, holding us here till that storm hit. You want to spike any Ermine's gun on that score, why, you just start with me."

Christy tensed, glancing quickly at Jack. Now it happens, she thought. But Heath only smiled; he flicked a match alight on his thumbnail and touched it to his cheroot. "Ah," he murmured, "the old clan fealty never falters. Charming. But recriminations are rather futile now, aren't they? Assuming that even the sawdust brains of an Ermine can grasp that elemental fact, I'd suggest we save our energies for dealing with the problem at hand."

Dallas Redmile moved between the two men casually, not looking at either of them. "How you size it, Cherokee? Any chance o' catching up them horses?"

The half-breed shrugged. "We go look, mebbeso. But I think no good. Long gone, horses, hours gone. The sand, she's cover all the track."

"Well, then," Dallas said quietly, dryly, "reckon on a maybe that sizeable, we best not waste our strength looking. There's Tubac over by the border, closest place I know of we might get horses. We got a full canteen of water apiece, that's something. Will hold us for a day or so. Got two horses for two people. They can ride to Tubac and fetch back mounts for the rest."

Heath rubbed his chin. "It'll be chancy, old pal.

There's law at Tubac, and I'd wager it has the word on us. Even a pair of strangers who ride in might be seized and questioned. And if even one person in the place could identify either of 'em . . . ."

"Well, reckon my face be the least known. And Christy, ain't nobody likely to spot her. Supposin' ole Jamison the prospector and his she-whelp handle this job? Seems the best bet, Jack."

"Un momento," Miguel put in. "Maybe there's a better way, eh? A cousin of mine, he got a place over east on the San Cruces, little ways above the border. He raise horse to sell. Is a longer ride than Tubac. But a couple of us start now, we get back tomorrow night with the horses, I think."

"This cousin," said Heath. "He knows all about you?"

"Si," Miguel grinned. "All. But he is the son of my mother's brother. His little boy is name' after me. He sell us horses and keep his mouth shut, *jefe*. His *vaqueros* too, they say nothing."

"Good, good. That's settled. We'll set out at once, you and I. . . ."

"Cap'n," Trask Ermine said gently, "you don't ride out of here with that poke of money. Not before we split on it, you don't."

"Did I say I was?" Heath clucked his tongue sadly, shaking his head. "No trust. That's the trouble with this trade. Absolutely no one trusts an honest thief. Get those saddlebags, Dallas, and we'll set about satisfying the common avarice."

154

Dallas brought the saddlebags, hunkered down, and spilled the packets of greenbacks out on the sand. With everyone watching, he counted out the notes by denominations, an equal share to each of the men and Christy.

"There you are, Trask," said Heath. "Exactly as we agreed. Satisfied?"

Ermine bent down and picked up a stack of greenbacks and handed it to Cherokee. He handed two more to his brothers and then straightened up, pocketing his share.

"I'm satisfied. I surely hope you are, Cap'n, for that settles our bargain, far as I'm concerned. Soon as you get back with them horses, we are dusting out of here. We ain't doing it in your company. That understood?"

"You strike me to the quick, Trask. You really do. Haven't I dealt on the square with you fellows?"

"Yeah, in a backhanded way," Trask said softly. "You just rub me against the fur, Cap'n. You're hard-nosed when there's no call, then you laugh up your goddam sleeve at a man. I don't like that. I don't like you. So we'll just call it quits hereafter."

"Soon as I've brought you horses, don't you mean?"

"Yeah, that's what I mean. You won't run no sandy either, not with your woman and Redmile left with us."

"Why, that's quite perceptive of you, Trask," Heath said with open sarcasm. "You'll get your horses, you and your rancid brotherhood. You'll pay for 'em out of your shares, too."

The Ermines and Cherokee pulled off by themselves,

155

while Christy and Dallas helped Heath and Miguel ready their gear and saddle up. They packed their bedrolls, some provisions, and a canteen of water each.

"How's your arm doing, Miguel?" Christy asked.

"Ha. It hurt some, but I'm think it be good enough." The Mexican chuckled. "I don' ride on my arm."

"What about your leg, Jack?"

"Better than it was. I'll hold up all right."

"I hope so. You think we might have a minute together?"

Heath nodded. "I mean us to, angel. Let's find some privacy. . . ."

They walked down the arroyo till they were cut off from the others. Then they stopped; Heath reached for her, but she pressed lightly away from his arms.

"Jack, what will you do with the boy when we get to the border?"

He smiled crookedly. "Angel, I'm just not of a mood for talking about boys."

"All the same—" She tightened her arms against him, holding him back. "We'll talk about it."

"What he deserves, after yesterday, is to have his neck wrung. I don't like a man roughing you about."

"I don't cotton to it myself," she said dryly. "But I can't blame him for trying to get away. So would you, if you felt like a lone virgin in a gang of rapists. Never felt that way myself, of course. . . ."

Heath threw back his head and laughed. "All right, angel. Have it your way. No harm letting him go free, I suppose . . . at the border." He eyed her quizzically.

"You haven't let that kid get under your skin, have you?"

Christy felt her face warm a little. "Well, you know I was a mother once. Not for long, but I know the feeling."

He laughed again. "You're saying the lad touches your maternal wellsprings? Well, so long as that's all he touches. . . . Funny thing with you, Christine. You've never really lost those nice shiny stars in your eyes, have you?"

"I dunno. . . . I suppose in a way not. I suppose I'd like to stop sometime. Just stop and live awhile. Haven't you ever thought of stopping, Jack?"

"Never for long, angel. To keep moving, to keep going always. That's all of living, for me. You know that."

"I know. But why is it?"

"Does it matter? Call it excitement. Call it a living. Call it any damned thing you please." He smiled, but his eyes were hard and unamused. "You haven't talked like that before. How deep does it go, Christine? Are you thinking of cutting loose?"

"Who doesn't, sometimes? When there's one too many stones in the beans. One too few drinks left in the canteen. Sure, I think about it."

"Perfectly all right. To think about it."

Again the smile streaked white across his dark face. His hands reached and settled lightly on Christy's supple waist, then sleeked down over the swelling flare of her hips. Gently, insistently, those hands pulled her

157

in until the tips of two firm, pointed breasts nudged against his chest. As always, the hard animal vitality of him sent a taut throb of desire through the girl.

She threw her head back, lips parting. "Jack," she whispered. "Oh Jack. . . ."

He kissed her shut eyes, her nose and cheek and the hammering pulse in her throat. Then his mouth sought the wide soft lips. For a time Christy let herself surrender to the fierce sweetness of lovers' kisses. Then she twisted determinedly against his arms and pulled free.

"Don't get carried away, boy. Not now and not here."

"Why not?" he chuckled. "All right. There'll be time, plenty of time. . . ."

Christy stood at the edge of the lava beds, watching Heath and Miguel ride toward the southeast. When a lopsided dune cut them from view, she turned back toward the camp, feeling a kind of weary despondency.

There was, she knew, no way of changing Jack Heath. Other women—he'd never been shy about letting her know—had tried it before her. You went along or you dropped out. I want to stop, she thought, so bad I can taste it, but I want him too. Oh, damn damn damn!

Dallas had untied Jason Drum, letting him sit on the ground and rub feeling back to his mangled wrists. Dallas sat on a rock a few yards away, idly holding a gun on him. She walked over and halted by Jason, saying stonily, "You'll be set loose. Jack give his word. Think you can manage to be a good boy till then?

Because if you cut any more capers, you'll be a dead one sure."

He lifted his head, eyeing her silently.

"You're welcome," she said coldly.

"Thanks."

He said it with a soft irony that surprised her a little. He wasn't a good-looking kid, but his eyes, dark and oddly brooding, got to her somehow, as they had from the first. Dallas gave her one of his dry, probing looks. Turning away, she was aware that her face was warming again. Damn them, she thought, suddenly and bitterly unsure of herself; damn all men.

XII

The storm was over; but the dust-laden sky continued to diffuse the sun's rays into a sallow glow, and it threw a silent gloom over the camp as the day wore on. A fire was built and some grub was cooked. Jason felt a little better after he was given something to eat and a few swallows of water. Then Dallas tied his hands again, but not so tightly, and left his legs free so he could walk slowly up and down under Dallas's watchful eye. They'd take no more chances with him, but it didn't really matter; he was still so sore from the beating that any wish to attempt escape was pretty well dampened. It seemed his best hope was to follow Christy's advice and not tempt the outlaws' anger again. If Heath had given his word to free him eventually, he might as well accept it as the best of bad choices.

There was nothing to do now but wait, and the Ermine brothers began to chafe with waiting. Pete and Clayt broke out bottles of whiskey, taking long slugs of the stuff that did nothing to sweeten their dispositions. Both were growing ugly and restless. Trask merely walked up and down, smoking one cigarette after another, and staring off toward the saffron horizon. Cherokee stretched out on the sand, tipped his hat over his face, and went to sleep. Christy and Dallas kept apart from the four of them, remaining on one side of the camp with Jason.

"I hope to God Jack and Miguel don't delay getting back," Christy muttered. "Sooner we're shed of this crew, the better."

"Yeh, they're a sore-footed lot." Dallas dug out his stubby pipe and chewed the stem ruminatively. "Course Jack didn't help matters none, rubbing 'em all ways to Sunday."

She smiled thinly. "Seems he just can't help himself."

Clayt Ermine came lurching their way. He halted and looked carefully at Christy, his eyes inflamed and out of focus. He said, "Have a drink," and held out his bottle.

"Go away," she said coldly.

"It's gonna be a cold wait, Red. You oughta warm up a little."

"Listen, you miserable—"

"Clayt!" Trask Ermine's voice came flat and warning. "No more of that. You hear me?"

160

"Hell with you, big brother. I do what I goddam feel like."

Trask came stalking across the camp. He grabbed the bottle away and flung it against a rock. Then he doubled up Clayt's shirtfront in both hands, shaking him. "Damn your weasel guts, we got enough troubles! You ain't stirring up more!"

He flung Clayt stumbling back across the camp, hustling him along with a hard kick. Walking over to Pete then, Trask held out his hand. "Let's have it." There was a dangerous edge on his tone, and Pete silently and sullenly handed over his bottle. Trask sailed it into the rocks.

"I can handle my snake juice all right," Pete grumbled. "Wa'n't no call for that."

"That's right. Hell, you don't need hooch in you to go on a pizen-eyed mean. It just gets you worse. You two got ants in your asses, why'n't you go hunting or something?"

Pete blinked owlishly. "What we hunt for?"

"Some brains, maybe. Hell, I don't know. Ask Cherokee."

The half-breed lifted his hat off his face. "You want hunt? Bighorn, maybe antelope?"

"Bet your ass," said Pete. "But I ain't see no game like that about."

"Plenty track around tanks before sand come. Plenty game water here, but not come when man around. You want hunt, you walk. Maybe walk long time, we find game."

"Good," Trask grunted. "We'll walk, then. Get our edges off, maybe get some meat into the bargain."

Clayt had slumped down on his heels, rubbing his belly. He had a sickly look. "You men go on. I don't feel good."

"Jesus," said Trask, shaking his head wearily. "I knew it. All right, get it up if you can. Then you best take to your blankets and sleep it off. Heath gets back, we are losing no time dusting away from here. Don't want you dragging along sick. Recall once you drunk too much shitty rotgut, you was sick for three days."

Clayt didn't reply. He climbed to his feet and went hunching away, his head down. Off behind some rocks, he began retching sickly. Pete gave a coarse chuckle and picked up his rifle, checking the action. "Let's get hunting, all right? Man, my mouth's watering already. Could put away 'bout a dozen juicy rump steaks by myself."

"You could put away the whole carcass yourself, you damn hog," said Trask. He watched Clayt come trudging back and throw himself on his bedroll. "You be all right, kid?"

Shuddering, Clayt pulled the blankets around him. He managed a nod.

"We fetch you back a nice feed, kid," leered Pete. "Ha-ha! Good juicy rump steak, how's 'at sound?"

Trask gave him a savage prod. "Come on, let's go. Cherokee, you lead out. Find us some track."

The three of them tramped away. For a while there was silence, except for Clayt giving out a muffled

162

groan now and then. Finally Christy yawned. "Dunno why, but somehow all this has made me very sleepy."

"Catch yourself some shut-eye," said Dallas. "I'll keep a watch. Till Jack gets back, might be a good thing if one or t'other of us is allus awake. We can spell each other, how 'bout it?"

"Considering the company, I call that a dandy idea, old booger."

Christy spread her blankets in the shade and lay down. Dallas said, "Got your kinks worked out, kid?" Jason nodded. "Catch some sleep yourself, then. Anyway sit down. Sight o' bother watching you on your feet."

Jason stretched out. He felt drowsy almost at once, warmth of sun and sand working into him. And he dozed. He wasn't sure for how long. A sharpness of voices roused him. He raised his head. Dallas had gone to sleep, head resting on his shoulder, and Jason's gaze moved past him.

Clayt Ermine was kneeling by Christy, and she was pulling away from him. He laid a hand on her. "C'mon, Red, you know what a man needs, you been up the hill and down again. Hell, you been shaking it at ever'body in camp. C'mon now, be nice to a man, nobody got t' know. . . ."

"Get away from me, you drunken slob!"

Her hand fetched Clayt a slap across the jaw that jolted him back on his heels. The pistol-shot impact of it made Dallas's head jerk up. "Huh? . . ."

Clayt lurched to his feet, holding his jaw. His drink-mottled face wore the imprint of the blow, one hard enough to half-sober him. Slowly his look changed from disbelief to hot rage.

"You barnyard bitch!" he bawled. "You get what-for now, by God!"

Abruptly Christy squirmed sideways out of his reach, trying to get to her jacket and the gun a couple yards away. Realizing her intent, Clayt made a stumbling dive; he pinned her flat to the ground. Dallas, on his feet now, was moving toward them with a stiff haste. He jammed his rifle into Clayt's back.

"Quit that! Get off her, you bastard, or I'll open you up like a can o' tomaters. . . ."

Clayt rolled half-upright, his face twisted in a mindless snarl. Suddenly his hand shot out and grabbed the rifle, twisting the barrel aside. Then he was fully on his feet, wrestling Dallas for the weapon. Wrenching it from the old man's frail hold, he knocked him staggering. Dallas kept his feet, and then he went back to the attack like a feisty terrier.

Clayt swung the rifle up and down, smashing the butt against Dallas's head. It was a full-armed blow dealt with crushing force. Dallas reeled aside, took a couple of faltering steps, and fell on his face. He lay with arms and legs flung out, his body twitching.

Jason sat up, savagely twisting his wrists against the ropes. Christy screamed and went for the jacket again. Wheeling around, Clayt flung the rifle aside and seized a handful of her hair. As he hauled her to her feet, she turned on him, kicking and clawing. Clayt held her

164

away one-handed, pulled back his other hand, and gave her a wicked clout. Half-stunned, she sagged down against his hold.

Jason quit fighting his ropes. He braced his back to a rock, pulled his heels up beneath his rump, and shoved himself upright. Clayt's back was partly turned to him. Jason balled his whole body and barreled at him in a low lunge. Clayt caught movement from the tail of his eye; he let go of the girl and started coming around, too late. Jason's head was sunk tight between his shoulders; he turned one shoulder for the impact as he slammed side-long into Clayt.

His weight knocked Clayt sprawling. Unable to halt his momentum, Jason tried to hurdle the downed outlaw but tripped and went down across him. Clayt heaved Jason's legs away and scrambled to his feet. His hand dived for the knife at his hip. Jason kicked wildly; his heel cracked against Clayt's shin and drove his leg from under him, Clayt hit the ground again, spun on his side to get clear of Jason, and then sprang to his feet. He whipped out the knife.

Desperately throwing his strength into one muscle-cracking effort, Jason surged up onto his heels. He straightened his legs and floundered up, tottering wildly for balance. In that instant Clayt took a long step, his knife snaking in and out. Jason felt his shirt tear and the burn of cold steel; he saw Clayt's red-streaked blade pull back for another thrust.

Jason leaped blindly aside, still off balance, and his foot struck Dallas's leg. He fell heavily, lit on his side, and then twisted over on his back as Clayt came after him.

Jason lashed out with both feet, but Clayt kept just out of reach, swiftly circling now. Not quite as helpless as an upended turtle, Jason tried to turn with him, but he couldn't turn quickly enough. He jerked his head away from Clayt's vicious kick, but it caught him at the joining of neck and shoulder.

It flooded his brain with a black pain that was sickening, literally paralyzing; for a moment he couldn't see. He lay helpless, open to the knife thrust he expected.

Then gun-roar filled Jason's ears. He felt the jolt of a falling weight.,

When he could see again, he realized that Clayt Ermine's body lay crumpled across him. Christy stood there, looking dazed as she lowered her pistol. She had shot Clayt in the back of the head.

Jason heaved upward; ragged pain blazed in his side. He pushed up again, and this time succeeded in rolling Clayt off him.

Dallas quivered and groaned. Christy dropped the pistol and fell on her knees beside him. She managed to turn him on his back. Dallas lifted his head; blood streamed down his face, but more than a blow on the head had felled him. He was hemorrhaging; blood flecked his lips. His eyes seemed remote and sunken as they looked toward Clayt's body.

"Don't mind me . . . sister . . . get out. Get out o' here . . . or you be dead . . . boy too."

166

His head sagged back.

"Dallas!" Christy wept. She shook him by the shoulders. "Dallas!"

Jason maneuvered slowly and laboriously to his knees. "Cut me loose," he said huskily.

She didn't seem to hear him. He yelled the words. She looked at him blankly and then, moving in a daze, came over and sliced away his ropes. Staggering to his feet, Jason stood swaying dizzily.

"He's done. We got to get out of here."

"We? . . . ." Christy stared at him. "No."

She touched Dallas's face; its color was ebbing to a slow grayness. "I can't just leave him, he's . . . he's not dead."

"He be dead in a little while. He's dying, can't you see that? We got no time to lose." Jason reached for a reserve of strength and raised his voice to a shout, hammering the words at her. "Didn't you hear what he said? They come back, we be dead people for sure! That shot'll fetch 'em—and you just killed their brother!"

As simple as that. There was nothing else to do, and the sense of it reached her then. As they hastily threw together two small packs of grub, water, and blankets, Jason's mind was working coldly. Packing light, they could carry two canteens of water apiece. Deliberately now, he gathered up the other canteens, unstoppered them one by one, and poured the water out. Then he hurriedly dumped all the excess grub on the ground and began savagely stamping it into the sand.

167

"They follow us," he muttered, "they'll do it dry and hungry."

Christy watched him dully. "They'll follow, you can bet on it. They'll follow us all the way to hell."

"It ain't far away, I reckon," Jason said grimly, bitterly. "I been living on the hot edge of it since I met you people."

He tramped over to Clayt, knelt down and ripped his shirt open, then uncinched the bulky money belt around the dead outlaw's waist.

Christy said shrilly, "What're you doing?"

"What's it look like? Getting what's mine. What I started out for."

"Oh sure, your money." She gave a harsh peal of laughter. "Your goddam money. Eight hundred seventy-five dollars! Not a cent less, right?"

It was easy to follow the tracks left by Heath's and Miguel's horses in the fresh-drifted sand. If there was any place of refuge close by, ranch or town or mining camp, neither Jason nor Christy knew how to find it. So they followed the tracks. On foot they couldn't hope to overtake the pair, but if they could keep ahead of any pursuit long enough, they might meet up with Heath and Miguel on their way back, maybe sometime tomorrow.

For about an hour they tramped at a hard, steady pace, hoping to pull a good lead. The big question was whether the Ermines and Cherokee would take up their trail at once, gambling on catching up before they got far, or whether they'd place first priority on finding food and water. Christy pessimistically allowed that they'd be in such a sweat to avenge their brother, they'd make the former choice. Even if they didn't, she pointed out, locating water and edibles might not take them long. Cherokee knew the country well, knew where good water could be found or dug for—perhaps along this same route. A tracker of uncanny ability, the half-breed could find game or improvise food from desert plants. At least he hadn't come on game by the time Clayt was killed; they'd heard no shooting.

The lemon-colored haze was fading, the sun burning low to the west. But darkness was still hours away, and Jason wondered if he could keep going that long. He had balled a piece of cloth torn from a blanket, pressing it tight to his side as he tramped along. Clayt's knife had entered shallowly between two of his ribs; he didn't think it was much of a wound. But it continued to bleed steadily, soaking the whole side of his shirt, then his trousers; finally he felt blood puddling in his boots.

Christy was watching him, and she said abruptly, "Let's stop. I'm going to tie that off."

Jason didn't argue. He peeled his shirt off and settled wearily on his hunkers, keeping an eye on their back-trail while Christy cut more strips from the blanket. Then she swabbed the wound clean. Opening a small sack of flour they'd packed along, she plastered hand-fuls of its cool whiteness over the cut. With the bleeding checked, she applied a thick compress to his side and tied it in place.

"That'll have to do you, boy. Afraid it won't help for long. What you need is rest."

Jason shook his head doggedly. "Got to keep going till dark. We don't know how close they are."

Christy straightened up and studied the sky. "Funny," she muttered. "The sun was clear awhile there, after the dust settled. Now it's darkening over again."

"Uh-huh. I think it might be brewing up a storm. A wet one this time."

"Just what we needed. Let's fix our stuff so it'll carry better, all right?"

They took the time to wrap their grubsacks in their soogans; tying them up again, they lashed their rifles to the outside of the blanket rolls. Slinging these compact bundles to their backs, they found the going a good deal easier.

They pushed on, scanning the back-trail often. The land was inclining slowly upward; its barren scape was rock studded and lifeless, except for more kinds of cacti than Jason had ever seen and, here and there, the spiky clustered canes of ocotillo. A black bulge of sheer rock grew out of the skyline ahead: a massive tilted shelf where the earth's crust had buckled in some bygone age, it formed a long rambling cliff that ran north and south. Didn't look as if it could be scaled, yet the tracks headed straight for it.

Meantime the heat had built oppressively, piling around them like layers of damp wool. A wind kicked up, hot and gritty. The clouds driving out of the west were swollen and dark bellied, and Jason guessed they

170

were in for a genuine cloudburst. There was no cover here, but there might be some up by that cliff.

Jason felt a weary drag in his muscles; he was growing light-headed. Pain shot knifelike through his side, and the wound was starting to leak again. He'd never last till dark, he knew. But he slogged on, letting Christy lead the way now.

Nearing the black cliff, they saw that several deep chasms split it from top to base. The horse tracks led into one of these. They entered it, finding themselves in a narrow defile whose rock-littered floor tended gradually upward. Its walls tapered so tightly overhead that the rims almost met. The place felt like a gloomy trap. Jason was glad when the sides widened out above, though the bottom of the cleft remained so cramped they had to proceed along it singly.

Thunder cannonaded, shaking the earth. The first fat raindrops fell. With unbelievable swiftness then, the sky split open and drenched them to the skin. In less than a minute the floor of the gorge was roiling with ankle-deep water.

"We better hustle," Christy said. "Come on, hurry it up!"

"What's the difference?" Jason said tiredly. "We're soaked through. . . ."

"It's a bad place for us, bub. You ever been caught in the open during one of these . . . an Arizona cloudburst? Well, I have. Flats miles wide covered with water in a few minutes. Think of that much water pouring into a little old gully like this, you can figure

171

what'll happen. But I never thought this damn gorge 'ud go on near so far. Come on, shake into it now."

The gorge bottom grew rougher and steeper as they climbed, and the water deepened at an alarming rate, cascading in torrents off the steep-sloping walls and funneling into the passage. As it swirled knee-high around their legs, Christy splashed to a stop. She whirled, grabbing Jason's arm. There was pure terror in her face.

"God, I can't even see the end of this thing, and we'll be rushed off our feet in another minute!" She yelled the words over the roar of thunder and water. "We got to climb . . . climb out of it. That way!"

She pointed at the rugged slant of one wall. It was a little less precipitous than the other, and by now the rimrock had tipped a lot lower, rounding off along its upper half. If they could make it that far, they'd be safe. But those few yards of treacherous lower wall might be unscalable unless they could lend each other a hand.

Jason sized up a ledge a couple feet above his head; it appeared solid enough. He didn't say anything, just pointed at it, then stooped and cupped his hands together. Christy set her heel in his palms; he boosted her as high as he could, then braced himself against her weight. The exertion slashed red pain through his side, and now the water was sweeping higher than his knees. From up-canyon came a sullen bellow as the full force of the flood came boiling down toward them. Once it hit, if he were still on his feet, he'd be carried away like

172

a cork, drowned or battered to death on the flinty walls.

Christy was clawing frantically at the ledge, trying to gain enough purchase to hike herself atop it. Her effort scaled away pieces of rotted stone that pelted down on Jason. "Hurry up!" he yelled. His arms numbed into his shoulders against the strain of her weight; the agony of his side blazed into his chest.

Then the weight left his hands, as Christy succeeded in scrambling onto the shelf.

A moment later, sprawled flat with only her head and shoulders showing, she thrust an arm down to Jason. He gripped her wrist; he found a slight foothold and began inching himself upward. He used Christy to steady rather than support him, picking holds with his feet and one hand carefully, knowing his full weight would yank her off the ledge.

The stub of rock broke under his foot; his holds slipped, and he dropped back into the water, falling to his knees. He was almost swept under before he fought back to his feet. The water reached nearly to his waist, and its increasing roar yanked his glance up-canyon. The flood's solid front was bucketing down toward him, raging and frothing between the walls.

Panic fed Jason's muscles as he seized Christy's arm again, barely picking his holds now as he climbed with a furious haste.

His free hand grabbed the projecting rock, and he clung desperately to it. Then Christy's other hand caught hold of that wrist. Crouched above him now, heels braced, leaning back to take his weight, she yelled "Hold on!" as the savage crush of water struck his body. It churned up to his waist, chest, armpits; it would have wrenched him away but for Christy's holds.

Then the first giant thrust of flood was past him, and Jason could partly brace himself against its powerful tug. The water climbed no higher, but for a frightening moment he wondered if Christy's strength would be enough to pull his body free of it.

For the moment it was all she could do just to hold on. Jason treadwheeled his legs wildly, trying to gain some traction with his feet. His right toes hooked solidly in a crevice; he pushed suddenly upward. Christy fell over backward, still gripping his wrists.

Inch by inch, fighting against a leaden exhaustion, he hauled himself up beside her.

For long moments they crouched in the driving rain, just resting. Then, holding onto each other, they tackled the last yards of the wall, which curved roughly inward now. After collapsing on the rimrock, they looked dazedly around them. The summit of this tilted height was a tortured jumble of rock wrenched loose by ancient convulsions, scarred and pitted by erosion.

Spotting a kind of hollow formed by the gap between two tilted slabs, they crawled over to it. Wedging themselves side by side within it, they were partly cut off from the slashing rain. There they huddled, shivering like a pair of drenched rats, and waited for the storm to play itself out.

XIII

Val Penmark and Anita Cortinas were crouched under an overhang in the lee of a high-shouldered ridge that pretty well cut off the blast of wind and rain. Taking shelter here before the storm had hit, they'd found a pack rat's nest that had yielded a good store of wood, enough to keep them supplied through the night. Their three horses, the paint mustang and two Apache ponies, had been restless and skittish when the thunder and lightning began, but the fire had its calming effect. Horses accustomed to campfires generally found something soothing in them, and Penmark hobbled the animals close in, so they could move toward or away from the fire.

Heading south away from the place where Penmark had ambushed the two Apaches, they had made good time. There was sound reason for wanting to, one of the Apaches having gotten away. Penmark had guessed, from the sheep carcass on their packhorse, that the pair had been sent out from Cayetano's band to get fresh meat. So the main bunch wasn't far away, and going by what he knew of Cayetano's habits, Penmark had figured it likely the war chief wouldn't find it inconvenient to seek retribution for the killing of a warrior of his. The one who'd gotten away would lead the band to the spot in no time. It was important for the good of the dead man's soul to see him properly buried; then they'd set out to punish the ones responsible. The sign would tell his comrades that one white-eyes had done the job and that his only companion was a woman. Overtaking the two would be a matter of pride and anger, for Apache war bands were small; a war chief couldn't afford the loss of even one seasoned brave. Since Cayetano was swinging generally back south anyway, it seemed a good guess he'd pick up the southward trail of his man's killer.

At least that was how Penmark sized it, and his blunt reasoning had convinced 'Nita too. She felt a numb terror of the Apache menace that might be dogging their trail, and she thought of the outlaws ahead of them. It was like feeling caught between two fires. But at least they had horses; they had plenty of food and water, and somehow the presence of the big grim-eyed gringo gave her a sense of assurance that helped keep fear in its place. His mad intent made her more than a little uneasy, but that was another thing.

Earlier today, they had seen the sandstorm from a distance, a brown shroud that yellowed the far sky, and Penmark had guessed it would blanket the whole region of Arrowhead Tanks well to north and south. But he knew the outlaws had been bound for there, remembering their mention of the place. So he wasn't greatly perturbed by the fact that sand would obliterate the track he'd followed this far. He knew where the Tanks were, not much over a day's ride now. If Heath's gang had gotten no farther before the storm came, he could pick up more sign from there, or maybe catch the outlaws still encamped there.

'Nita wasn't at all enthused by the prospect, but her mind had settled into a resigned fatalism by now. She had cast her lot with the big gringo's; she was willing to share his fate come what might, even die by his side if she must.

Wind snaked in beneath the overhang and guttered the fire, throwing a wild blend of light and shadow beyond its pocketing glow. Except for the occasional chill of wind, 'Nita felt snug and dry, and there was something companionable in the way the horses had pulled near, sharing an oasis of light and warmth with two humans. She and Penmark had made a good meal of wild mutton, frying strips of it in the skillet and wolfing it down hungrily. The meat was tough and greasy, it had a strong wild flavor she wasn't used to, but it was hot and filling as nothing she'd eaten in days had been. 'Nita felt stuffed and relaxed.

She made small rambling talk, telling Penmark of little things in her past life. Matters she might contemplate with sadness, but no longer with that first tearing sense of loss. So much had happened to her in a few days, a violent succession of events rocking her world apart, that already her past had blurred at the edges, taking on something of the unreality of a dream. Later it might all return with a bitter sharpness. But here and now, soothed by a sum of simple animal comforts, she could speak of trivialities with a wistful pleasure—of *Abuelito's* handskills with wood and leather, of a pet lizard she had once kept, of a red dress she'd prized and had liked to put on sometimes, though there were no holidays to celebrate and no company in which to wear it at lonely Corazon.

So she chattered idly, not knowing whether Penmark was listening or not. He stared at the silvery gouts of rain dripping from the overhang, never moving except to throw more wood on the fire. His thoughts were his own, grim and forbidding thoughts from his expression; but then his expression was always the same. Maybe he was thinking of how the rain could add to his tracking problems.

Talking in her own language gave a freer rein to her thoughts, and she knew that *el viejo's* Spanish was much better than her English. In their time together he'd unbent enough now and then to clarify in her own tongue a point which she found difficult to grasp in his, but always with a sour impatience that let her know he resented the doing. So they did nearly all their conversing in their own languages, and it worked surprisingly well.

'Nita could be just as stubborn, and also she enjoyed exercising her voice again. She was satisfied when, finally, she stirred a grunt of annoyance from him.

"I don't know it's so grand you lost that cinch on your tongue," he growled. "You ain't hardly quit wagging it."

"I like to talk. Is that so bad?"

"Best women know when to keep their mouths shut."

"When is that?" she asked innocently. "For you, *viejo,* I think that is never."

He hitched a cramp out of one haunch, scowling. "I

178

tell you one thing—I am getting a crawful of being called that. How'n hell old you think I am?"

"I think you are as old as *Abuelito* was. He was fifty-nine."

"I ain't no fifty-nine," Penmark growled.

"It must be you remind me of *Abuelito*." She smiled a little. "I did not think of that before, but yes, some ways you are like him."

"Jesus. Like *your* grandpa?"

"*Sí.*"

"I never been nobody's grandfather," he snapped, "and I sure to hell ain't yours."

"Maybe you were not lucky then."

"Ha!"

For a time the two of them were silent, looking out at the rainy murk. Except when sheets of skyfire lit up everything brighter than day, all objects such as trees and rocks were an anonymous blur. It was as if the storm and night had cut them off from the world. Somehow the feeling increased 'Nita's sense of security in this crude oasis of theirs. She wiggled her feet comfortably inside the tall Apache moccasins, very glad now that Penmark had forced her to wear them.

Not that the gesture had implied anything but a cold practicality on his part. He simply didn't want her slowing him down for lack of being decently shod. Whatever streaks of tenderness were in the man lay buried and unreachable, she was sure. At best he felt a sense of bitter obligation toward her, mixed with a fleck or two of guarded gratitude. He had no room for

179

any strong thought except vengeance on the man Jack Heath.

But I like him, she thought. I like this old gringo and I do not care what he thinks.

Penmark lowered his head so the brim of his hat put his face in deep shadow. Then he said slowly, "I tell you, I don't know what's going to happen in the next day or so. It is going to be a damn tight thing when I catch up with them men. And them 'Paches may be at our backs somewhere, we don't know how close. It is a damn bad situation for you."

"Do not blame yourself for that. I—"

"Hellfire!" His face came up, his eyes steely with anger. "Who said a whit about blame? Ain't my fault if you dealt into my affairs. All the same, I'm beholden to you."

"You owe me nothing," she said stiffly.

As if he hadn't heard her, he went on, "Soon as any trouble shows, if we find it or it finds us, what I'll do is try to hide you. Put you in a place you'll be safe. I can't do no more."

"I have a rifle," she said quietly. "I can shoot. *Abuelito* taught me to shoot."

He did not reply. After a half-minute of trying vainly to read past the hard set of his face, 'Nita gave up. She was tired; abruptly she realized how tired, and there was no more to say. . . .

After the rain had slacked off to a steady drizzle, Jason and Christy looked around for better shelter. They were wet to the skin and bitterly chilled, and their only thought for the moment was of a place to get warm and dry. It would be dark before long, and once night closed down, they would have to stay where they were till morning. If the Ermines and Cherokee were anywhere behind them, they'd be occupied with the same problems. Meantime the rain would have wiped out all track, and any way out of their dilemma would have to wait till morning.

They stumbled along the ragged rim of the pass that had almost claimed their lives, working across the tilted height till the gorge petered out. Then they were descending the far side of the vast rise, finding that it slanted off gradually on its east flank. But it was still rugged going, and the rain-slick rock made for treacherous footing. The gray daylight was starting to fade when Jason spotted what looked like the black mouth of a cave in the pitted scarp. They clambered over to it.

It was a cave all right, a fairly shallow one, so low-arched that even Christy had to bend over to enter it. But it was dry inside, floored with soft sand, and scattered with pack rats debris that would make a fire. Jason carefully beat every corner of the place with a stick in order to roust out any rats or snakes. Apparently there were no tenants in or out; the only animal droppings he found were old and powdery.

Christy had a packet of matches wrapped in oilcloth; it didn't take long to get a lively blaze going. When the two of them had thawed out, they peeled off their outer clothes and footgear and propped them on sticks by the fire. Their blanket rolls were dry enough, thanks to the waterproof tarp sheets they were wrapped in.

"We better look to that cut of yours," Christy said.

She knelt beside him and started to undo the bandage. Jason's face got warm; he said, "Uh, look, I'll take care of it."

"Stop fidgeting, dammit. You got your drawers on, haven't you?"

All the same, he didn't feel decently covered, and she wasn't by a far sight—not in a wet short-skirted chemise that hugged every nubile curve and hollow. But he sat still, looking self-consciously away as she peeled off the bandage. The compress was stuck fast to his flesh with blood-caked flour, and he gave a yowl as she jerked it away. Fresh blood welled over the livid edges of the wound. Christy washed it clean and bent close to inspect it, making him too aware of her body warmth.

"We got to close that off," she muttered. "There's something might help. Seen some of it growing close by this cave."

"What's that?"

"*Sangre de Cristo.* It's a plant with sap in it that dries quick. You can seal a wound with it. I'll fetch some."

Taking her knife, she stepped out in the rain. In a couple minutes she returned with a handful of half-coagulated fluid. The stuff burned like fury as she smeared it along the cut, but the bleeding was checked almost at once. As she put on another bandage, Christy said, "That ought to fix it all right. It's a clean wound,

182

not like a bullet 'ud make. Jack showed me that trick with the plant."

"He's a smart man."

"Oh, he's that," she said dryly. "He has more twists in him than a sidewinder." She touched his forehead. "You cooking up a little fever there, Mr. Drum. Let's wrap you up nice and comfy, and you get some sleep."

Jason nodded dully. He was shivering despite the fire's warmth; his head throbbed sickly and his belly churned. Blood loss and the ordeals of the past few days were catching up. Christy spread out a ground-sheet and a blanket and motioned him to lie down, afterward tucking a couple more blankets around him. Like a mother bundling up her infant, he thought, feeling downright foolish. But the feeling faded as a vast weariness crept over him. He shut his eyes. . . .

A fresh sputter and crackle of flames penetrated his last shred of consciousness, pulling his eyes drowsily half-open. Christy had dropped more wood on the fire, and now she straightened up. Standing sideways to him, she slipped the straps of her chemise off her shoulders; the wet garment slid down her legs and she stepped out of it.

For a heart-stopping moment he saw more naked loveliness than he had ever dreamed of. The high wash of flamelight made a pink witchery of the girl's creamy flesh, of her ripe and conical breasts stressed by two circling shadows, of the red-pink nipples tautly pointed from the rainy chill, of the flat belly and the flare of her mature hips, of the smooth beauty of her rounded

183

thighs and the secret darkness where they joined.

She was so for only a moment; then she picked up a blanket, threw it around her, and turned back to the fire. Jason quickly closed his eyes again.

For a while his sleep was plagued by a succession of bad dreams. Then he slept soundly. When he woke, it was suddenly, and he lay blinking at a hint of steel-gray light from the cave mouth. Then he raised his head. Christy was sitting cross-legged on the other side of the fire, fully dressed except for her moccasins.

"How you feeling?" she asked.

Jason sat up carefully and felt of his side. There was hardly a twinge of pain—and the bandage was dry. "Pretty good." He didn't quite meet her eyes. "Didn't you get no sleep?"

"Enough." She yawned and raised a hand to pat her close-cropped hair. "Much as I could with you sawing wood all this time. It's 'most daylight. You hungry?"

"Yeah."

"I cooked up some bacon and bannock." She nodded at the skillet beside him. "Go ahead. I ate. Our clothes are dry, 'cept for your boots and my moccasins. You got any ideas?"

Jason, about to set his teeth into a chunk of pan bread, gave her a wary look. "Uh, ideas?"

"Yes, like how we'll pick up Jack's trail. That rain pretty well done for his and Miguel's tracks."

He bit into the bread, frowning. "Maybe we ought to

stay where we are. They be back this way with the horses, won't they?"

"Sure, but meantime there's our three friends back there. Course our track's been wiped out too, and I doused the fire before it begin turning light so's they won't have any smoke to find us by. But they know the way we was going, and that damn Cherokee knows this country like you know your own bee-hee."

"We never raised no sight of 'em before the storm hit. Maybe . . ."

"That's a big maybe, boy. They could be closer than we know. Anyway, those damned Ermines will be out for blood—ours. And you can bank they will start looking soon's it's full light. This cave is close to the head of that pass, and they'll be coming through it. You want to gamble that half-Injun don't spot it and come looking?"

Jason shook his head dismally. God, he felt used up. He was rested and cool-headed again, but plain used up where it counted, in the mind and guts. These past days had been an on-running nightmare of chasing or being chased, more brutally harrowing business compressed into a week than he'd known in his life. It was a nightmare from which there was no pinching himself awake. Where would it end? How?

"I reckon, soon's there's light enough, we best try to get our bearings and move on."

"Right you are, Drum." Christy grinned and reached over to pat his hand. "Maybe we'll get lucky for a change. Go on, wrap yourself around that grub."

Jason ate in silence for a moment. Then he said, "How you fall in with him anyway . . . Heath?"

"You might call it my destiny. As Jack says, 'It was jolly well your destiny, old girl.' " She made a face, letting her shoulders lift and settle. "I dunno. Does it matter?"

"It matters, sure. I mean, I want to hear it."

She made a pretty sketchy account of it, so that mostly he had to read between the lines. Her folks had lived on a busted-down farm in Illinois, and she supposed it was hating dirt and poverty—as much as getting with child by a neighbor lad—that had made her run away from home when she was sixteen. She'd had a notion of heading California way, but penniless and making her way by hook or crook, as she vaguely put it, she hadn't gotten farther than Tombstone before her baby was born. Some kindly people had helped her, and she'd set out to repay them by taking a job as entertainer at the Lady Gay Saloon.

"I could of made lots more at one of the girls' boarding houses, and believe you me, there was plenty of 'em in that place, but . . ." She shrugged. "Somehow it never seemed worth it."

"Boarding houses?"

"Uh-huh. Take it your daddy never told you about boarding houses."

"I reckon I know what you mean."

"Well, that's quick and bright of you, Jason." She patted his hand again. "Anyway . . . oh, what's to tell? My baby was sickly, he died after a year. And I started drifting. One place and then another. I was a gambler's shill for a spell. Then I met Jack. I guess," her mouth gave an ironic twist, "it was love at first sight."

"I just don't see . . ."

"What don't you, honey?"

"How you can have a feeling for a man like that."

"You don't, huh? Well, you have a lot coming to you." Her green eyes went flinty; she pressed her palms together and gazed down at them. "It don't matter what you call it. When you have a man, you stick by him, no matter where he goes or what he does. You maybe don't like much of what he does or the places it gets you into, but that's how it is." She smiled bleakly. "How's that for a declaration of principles?"

"I guess you're right," Jason muttered, looking away from her. "I got a lot to learn."

"You have, bub, you really have. You don't know anything, do you?"

A gently teasing note in her voice made him look at her again. She was smiling a little, her eyes softening. Then she came to her feet and moved to his side; she knelt in a quick movement, laying her hands on his shoulders. "It's time you learned," she whispered, and tipped her mouth into his. The soft wetness drew his senses like a drug, and he reached for her then, awkwardly. It was an embrace that began gently and turned swiftly, fiercely passionate.

Christy drew back a little in his arms, her face flushed.

Her fingers brushed his cheek in a wondering,

187

strangely tender way. "Honey, haven't you ever held a girl before?"

"I guess I ain't. Not like this, I mean. I don't much know what's to do."

"What you do," she said huskily, "is go on doing and don't stop. Do it, Jason."

XIV

They had ridden steadily through the cool hours of false dawn. A little after sunrise they saw the black field of lava rock where Arrowhead Tanks lay. Penmark rode in slowly with his Sharps resting on his pommel, and 'Nita kept her rifle ready too. There was no smoke or other sign of life; nobody raised an alarm at their approach. They rode cautiously into the place and found it deserted.

The basins that had held water were filled with sand, 'Nita saw; sand had piled in deep fans against the rock slabs. People had been here after the sandstorm had swept over the place, as the wet char of a fire showed. But they had left before the rain came, for there was no other sign that she could see.

There was, however, the body of a man. It lay in its sodden clothing at one side of the sandy clearing between the tanks. Penmark dismounted and walked over to the body and bent down by it.

"Dead for a day anyways," he muttered. "Seems like somebody cracked his head for him."

"Do you know him?" 'Nita asked.

188

"Dallas Redmile."

The name meant nothing to her, and Penmark didn't trouble to enlighten her. He began walking back and forth over the damp ground, his face set like iron. From the tension of his body 'Nita sensed the frustration and rage he felt. Where had the people he was looking for gone from here? The question would be tearing at him. She wished he might call it quits now, give up his mad quest, but she had no real hope that he would. He was a man driven; if he had to continue his search on blind guesswork, he'd do so.

He halted by a shallow mound that more or less blended into the rain-pounded texture of the surrounding earth. "Now," he murmured, "what's this here look like to you?" Not waiting for an answer, he heeled the butt of his rifle deeply into the mound. "Pretty loose. I lay odds someone's been planted here, and inside the last day or so."

"Maybe," 'Nita said uneasily, "it is only sand piled up by the wind."

"Now that might be, sis. It just might."

Penmark knelt down and started digging with his hands. Shock held 'Nita silent for a moment, and then she said softly, "But you will not desecrate the dead—if it is a grave."

"If it's a grave, somebody's in it," he grunted, pitching out handfuls of dirt. "I aim to see if that somebody's Jack Heath."

'Nita stepped to the ground and led her paint off a little way, keeping her back to Penmark. She did not

189

want to see what he found. No good could come of disturbing the dead. The grave wasn't very deep; presently she heard him cease to dig, but she did not look around. If there was a body, she hoped it was not that of the young gringo Jason Drum. After a minute she heard a sound of earth being thrown back in the hole. She came slowly to Penmark's side as he carelessly finished mounding up the dirt again and stood up.

"Well, it ain't Heath. 'Pears to be one of the Ermine brothers. Never met none of 'em, so can't be sure. . . ."

"But two are dead. Why did they bury the one and not the other?"

Penmark rasped a hand across his gray-stubbled jaw. "Can't be sure of nothing, 'cept there was a fight here. This boy now, he got shot to death. Could be him and Redmile was on different sides. Or they had a falling out of some kind and done for each other, though that don't seem likely." He shrugged. "Your guess is good as mine."

"How will you find the people now?"

The bitter stubbornness etched harder into his face. "They left here before the rain or sometime after it started. Wherever they was when it stopped, they begin making sign again."

"But you do not know which way they went."

"They was going south to the border. I hazard they went on that way—straight south."

"The rain lasted a long time. If they rode on while it rained, they went a long way before it stopped."

He gave her that iron look. "Wasn't much daylight left when the rain started. Night was pitch dark. I don't reckon they traveled much last night. My guess, we're closer to 'em than we been yet. All right, be easy to miss their track where it picks up, even so. But south's a good guess, and that's where we're going."

As he spoke, his gaze swung north across the glittering flats they had crossed. The Apaches he believed were on their trail would be coming south too. Yesterday the two of them had sought shelter soon after the storm had begun. Though the Apaches ignored physical discomfort, they wouldn't stir while darkness held. They weren't likely to decamp till shortly before sunrise. So she and the gringo had a good lead on the Indians, 'Nita thought. But it would not help them that the sandstorm and later the rain had broken their trail in a couple of places, for the Apaches too would know of Arrowhead Tanks; and coming south to that favorite camp, they would find the trail once more if they had not picked it up again earlier.

Perhaps it was premonition, perhaps only her own terror of Apaches; whatever, a sinking dread gnawed at 'Nita. For her and the gringo, for others too, this bright day might be *Dia de los Muertos*. It was a custom in old Mexico to hold a festival of the dead in order to mock Death, to show a human scorn of Death. But behind such mockery lay the shape of fear, a fear she could strongly taste.

The Day of the Dead. So it might prove to be.

Without more words they mounted and rode away

191

from the lava field, holding the rising disc of sun to their direct left. 'Nita rode behind the gringo, watching the high set of his shoulders. What is the good of this? she thought despairingly. It would be such an easy thing to miss the track he sought. Yet find it or not, he would never stop. She had a vision of them riding a hot wasteland forever. . . .

Penmark pulled up. He had been scanning the land and the sky unceasingly, and now he was looking east, into the sun.

'Nita blinked several times against its blinding rays before she made out a smudge of smoke mounting against the sky. Penmark swung his horse that way now, and she reined alongside him.

"You were looking for smoke?" she asked.

"For smoke, for any likely thing. Wonder if a fire got laid just now or if I missed it before on account of the sun in my eyes."

"But would they go that way . . . east?"

"Sis, I don't know a damn thing. But it's worth following up."

The smoke was thinning away, and then its wispy banner showed no more. Penmark kept on, never turning his eyes from the distant hill that had marked its source.

They rode perhaps an hour while the sun climbed higher. It was out of their eyes by the time they reached the sharp rise of land. Halting at its summit, they looked down into a steep draw whose sides were covered with heavy brush and boulders. A trickle of smoke

192

still rose from the remains of a fire, but nobody was in sight. Penmark dismounted and led the way to the pebbly bottom of the draw. Someone had thrown sand on the fire, but it must have smoldered a long time before it died.

Penmark began sorting out sign. Three men had been here, he said, two of them booted, one wearing moccasins. They had sheltered here during last night's storm, had dried out by the fire after the rain let up, and had gone on maybe a couple or three hours ago. This much he was able to read from the well-trampled ground around the fire, but it took him several minutes to find where, among the flanking rocks, the men had left the draw and resumed their trek.

The trail pointed eastward. But the surprise was all three men had been afoot.

"Are they the ones you look for?" the girl asked.

Penmark cuffed back his hat and scratched his head. "Maybe. Three of 'em anyway. But that don't spell out right. Less Redmile and the Ermine kid, it still leaves four people unaccounted for. Heath, his woman, a Mex, a half-breed, two Ermines, the Drum kid. That's seven. None of these three was a woman, that's all I'm sure of. And what the hell happened to their horses? They had extra saddle mounts, packhorses too. Nary a horse with this bunch."

He stood a moment staring bleakly at the ground, his jaw clamped.

"Maybe," 'Nita ventured, "these are not any of them, *viejo.*"

"Dammit, how many white men you going to find in this country at any time? It's got to be them, three of 'em. Something happened back at the Tanks. There was a fight, we know that part. I aim to find out the rest of it."

He climbed back to his saddle and took up the track of the three men, going eastward. But it was slow going; the way led over flinty and boulder-strewn terrain. Penmark sweated and cursed under the climbing sun. The hours were trickling away, and so was the precious time he had gained.

The land ahead sloped gradually up to a black cliff that seemed to run for miles north and south. They followed the trail through a tight gorge that cut upward through the cliff, petering out on its other side in a gentle slant. The country beyond continued rugged and broken up, but now the track showed plainer.

As they proceeded down the long slant, Penmark halted with a sharp oath. Stepping to the ground, he examined the ground closely.

The track of the three men had crossed another trail. Ahead of them, two other people had come off this long height and had proceeded east. A man and a woman. The woman had been wearing moccasins, and Penmark identified her as Heath's woman, the girl called Christy. Who the man was, he couldn't be sure. A good-sized fellow; might be Heath himself.

Anyway, the track of the three men had crossed onto theirs and was now following it. Penmark, wearing a fresh spur on his anger, pushed along hard and fast.

The trail was the whole focus of his attention, and it was 'Nita who kept her eyes open on every side. Her sense of apprehension was deepening, and nothing that happened now would surprise her very much.

The land rose and fell in irregular patterns so that she couldn't see very far ahead or behind. It wasn't till they came atop a ridge that she was able to see a long way to their rear. Now she saw at once some moving dots that were riders, a number of them coming down the now-distant grade where the trails had crossed. Here they were clustering and then stopping, as if to inspect the new sign.

"Look, *viejo* . . ."

Penmark quartered his horse around and looked. Then he swore quietly and shook his head.

"I had a hope of sorts," he muttered. "Hoped if them 'Paches was behind us and found our trail again, they might give up once we turned east. No such luck, though, once they seen how fresh it was. We're sky-lined, girl. Let's get off of here."

They rode down the far side of the ridge; Penmark urged a quicker pace. Trying to hold alongside him, 'Nita cried, "What will we do?"

"Like I said I'd do if trouble found us. Hide you. Don't know if that can be managed, but I'll try."

Some minutes later they rode into a crooked valley, which must have been carved out long ago by a stream that twisted down its center like a sparkling snake. Last night's rain had raised the water so that the creek roiled briskly and widely overflowed the valley floor in many places. Ages of weathering had worn most of the valley to bare shale, which was rotted and crumbling, studded with huge outcrops. Here and there where loose soil had blown into gaps and crevices, scrubby vegetation had taken root.

Penmark hauled up and looked around, studying the whole landscape. "This here's as good a place as any. You keep right behind me, hear?"

He reined into the shallow creek and turned upstream. Its bed was crumbled shale that would leave no sign at all. But it could not go on so forever, and then they would have to leave the water. Knowing they had gone upstream or down, all the Apaches would have to do was split their force.

As the valley rode toward its upper end, deltas of sand sloped in broad slashes to the water's edge. Penmark, leading the packhorse, abruptly swung out of the stream and up one such sandy bank. 'Nita followed him till they climbed their horses onto a naked shale ledge, and there Penmark halted. She looked back in dismay at the plain tracks their three animals had left in the sand. Then Penmark stepped down and broke off a branch of scrub next to the ground.

He crossed the sand to where they'd left the water, then began walking backward, carefully brushing the hoofprints smooth. Every couple feet he stopped, gathered up handfuls of the fine sand, and sifted it lightly over the brush marks. Now she understood. Leaving the water on solid rock, they would have left wet traces and fresh shale nicks that the Apaches could not miss.

A sifting of dry sand would cover every particle of sign clear to the ledge.

When Penmark was done, a five-yard belt of unmarked sand lay between them and the stream.

'Nita said, "You think that will fool them?"

Penmark shook his head tiredly. "Sis, I don't know. They'll look for us to leave the water on a rock stretch. All we can gamble is they won't figure on no trick like this. On account of they look close, they'll see things you and me would never spot. From here on, even if we stick on rock, we'll leave sign. What we got to hope, they won't look too far off the bank. Let's move on. We got to find a place for you to lay up."

Afoot and leading their horses, the two moved northerly across the hot shale beds, trying now to avoid treading on sand. They worked slowly up the valley's boulder-littered north slope, and Penmark didn't pause till they reached the rim. Here he stopped, pulling the horses around back of a massive outcrop. Crouching behind it, he sighted down a crack between two jags of rock.

"This'll do. Now listen." He looked at her, talking slowly and spacing his words. "Keep your head down and watch through this slot. You can make out the whole valley. When they come, no matter what they do, you stay put less'n you see 'em come up that bank where we left the stream and then start up this way. Then you'll know they cut our sign, so you fork that nag of yours and run for it. Otherwise, you stay set till they are gone. I can't tell you where to go then. Maybe—"

197

Stiff-backed at being spoken to as a child, she snapped, "That does not have to be your concern."

"Suit yourself." He started to turn away.

"But you . . . you will not stay?"

"Told you I was looking to hide you, that's all. This here's as safe as I can make it for you. Me, I'm hustling on that trail I was on before it goes cold. Come this close, I don't aim to lose those birds now."

'Nita caught hold of his hand. "Wait, *por favor!* If the Apaches find nothing here, they will go on. They will follow the other trail, yes? The one left by the *ladrones* you seek?"

"Sure they will. Only I'll be well ahead of 'em. Heath's bunch, they're on foot. I'll catch up fast now."

"And then the Apaches will come."

"Then," he said impatiently, "it won't matter. Time they catch up, I'll be a dead man or Jack Heath will be. After that it don't matter a whit."

She held tight to his hand. "Not to you. But I will care. I will care very much."

Penmark stared at her for a long moment, then said softly, "Ah, Jesus." But he didn't try to pull his hand away. "Look, it won't do. I held on this far for just one thing. You know that."

"Yes, but it is wrong. It is wrong to think of nothing but to kill a man. It is wrong to throw away your life." She hesitated. "It is wrong for you to leave me here."

"Sure, that's the most of it. You're scared."

"For you," she said simply.

Penmark growled wearily, "Ah, for Christ's sake,"

198

and pulled his hand away from hers, then tramped to his horse.

"*Viejo,* wait," she said desperately. "Suppose that you wait here with me till the Apaches have gone. Where will they go?"

He gave her an impatient glance. "You said it. They'll go on that trail those fellows left, they'll . . ." He broke off; understanding flickered in his face. "What you're saying, they will hit Heath and his men."

"Won't that be a better thing than for you to fight so many *ladrones* alone? Let them fight the Apaches first. Then, I think, there won't be so many *ladrones.*"

"Then you 'n me follow the 'Paches, huh?" Penmark took off his hat and sleeved his sweaty face. " 'Paches might even get Heath. Leastways they'll make it easier for me to get him. Well, by God now. I think we'll just do it your way, sis."

"Ah, but I have forgotten. The young gringo, your friend. If he is with them—"

Penmark shook his head grimly. "Drum'll just have to take his chances. Like enough they done for him already and dumped his body in a canyon some'eres. Anyways there's more'n him to think about."

'Nita wondered if he meant her; she hoped so.

"You got any of that petticoat o' yours left?"

"*Sí.*"

"All right, you tear that up and blindfold the horses. Horse with his eyes covered won't let a whicker out of him. I don't want 'em making no signals to them Apaches' ponies."

Penmark tramped back to the outcrop and, sitting on his heels, watched the valley through the eyeslot he'd chosen. 'Nita wriggled out of her petticoat. It was a filthy remnant of the garment it had been, but enough of it remained for her to tear it into three strips with the aid of her claspknife. She tied the pieces around each horse's head.

Afterward she sat down in the warm shade of the outcrop, her back against it, and shut her eyes. A trembling ran through her; she felt as spent as one who had run a hard race. Or was it a battle she had won? She had made this tough gringo listen. Perhaps she had even brought him to an awareness of something other than his own mad purpose.

Yes. A battle won.

"Listen, girl. . . ."

She opened her eyes.

Penmark wasn't looking at her; his gaunt profile showed nothing. "Tell you what . . . if we come out of this alive." He cleared his throat harshly. "I got a place outside New Hope. You want to come and stay there, you're welcome."

It was hard to believe what he was saying, harder to steady her voice. "If you are sure—"

"Well, Jesus, yes. I wouldn't a offered otherwise."

He sounded very cranky. A half minute went by before she ventured to say more. "I am a good worker. I can keep a good house for you and I can cook—"

"Hell, I'll spoil my own grub 'fore I fry my guts with Mex cooking." After a stiff silence, he said as if in grudging half-apology, "I got a Mex cook at the ranch. Pepe. He cooks pretty fair American for my crew. Lay odds you never had no schooling."

"No, *Señor*." Whispering it.

"Well, there's a good enough school in New Hope. You'll want some clothes and fixings like a girl should have. Dolores, that's Pepe's wife, she'll lend you a hand with all that fooferaw. I don't know a shuck about it."

'Nita closed her eyes again. She didn't dare to say anything. He would be roughly sardonic, she was sure, to any word of thanks; therefore she would say nothing. At least not yet.

"They're coming," Penmark muttered.

Standing up, she peered around the edge of the out-crop. The Apaches were riding swiftly down the west slope of the valley, clattering across the sun-blasted shale to the edge of the flashing stream. Here they stopped; there was discussion. Then one of them, a big man, pointed up and down the creek. Promptly the band split apart, half of the men riding upstream, the rest following the creek toward the valley's south end.

"Damn it, pull your head back," Penmark growled. "Better yet, get over by the horses, hold 'em ready. Might have to light out of here fast. We will know damn shortly. . . ."

XV

Jason and Christy had been hiking since early dawn with no idea of whether they were on the right track. For all purposes, they were good and lost. They couldn't find their way to any habitation unless they stumbled on it by accident. The rain had wiped out Heath's and Miguel's tail. The sun had come up bold and brassy, and they held a roughly southeasterly direction by it; but there as little chance of their being on an exact line with the route that Heath and Miguel had taken.

Jason's side began to pain him, and he worried about the wound tearing open again. But he said nothing.

It was Christy who finally said it, "Look, this is no good. Let's stop and figure what we'll do."

Jason was glad to stop; his legs felt wobbly. He plunked himself on the ground and eased his meager pack off his shoulders. Christy sat down beside him and said, "I'd say we've pretty well had it, wouldn't you?"

"I'm all right."

"Bull. We're both of us just about used up. We can keep on going till we drop, and there's no sense to that. When they catch up, we'll be in no shape to stand 'em off."

Jason took a small drink from his canteen; he nodded morosely. "I guess that makes sense."

"Sure it does. Say we find us some good cover.

Something we can put our backs to. Then we can just rest and wait. They'll find us, but we can make a fight of it anyway."

Jason took in the terrain they were crossing. It was as rugged a stretch as he had seen, broken up by redrock mesas and lesser formations of all kinds, and he thought it unlikely that Heath and Miguel had crossed here. Miguel, knowing the country, might choose a better route. They could be going farther off-trail all the time, getting themselves more and more lost. It made sense to stop, and there was always a chance, however slight, that they'd lost the Ermines and Cherokee.

If they hadn't, they might as well wait for them.

"Let's get up higher," he said. "We'll want to see 'em coming."

They worked on an upward incline toward a high tilt of sandstone cliff. Much of its rimrock had crumbled away, forming a rough breastwork of splintered blocks along its base. The cliff rose in a concave arch so that the rim projected far out and a deep pocket lay between the fallaway rock and the cliff base. Snugged in that pocket, they had plenty of shade, a solid wall at their backs, and a solid overhang above their heads. From behind the breastwork they had a clear view of the rough but rolling terrain to the west.

No matter how anyone came at them, he could be seen a good ways off; he'd have no cross under their guns. Yet he might manage it by dodging from rock to rock, for the open stretch was littered with outcrops and loose chunks. He could work in damned close if he were willing to take his chances, then settle down to wait them out.

Christy echoed Jason's dismal thought. "We got water enough for two days," she observed. "Three at the most. That sun works around this side, it's going to fry us."

"At least we got water. They ain't."

"Don't bet on it, Jason. It'll only take one man to pin us here. The others'll be free to forage . . . and that damn breed, I believe, could turn up water in hell."

Jason checked over his Winchester and Christy's; he counted their supply of shells. They had fifty rounds of .45-.70 ammunition apiece. It was enough to last them for maybe as long as their water did, depending how hard they were pressed. After that it wouldn't matter.

There was one hope, and he voiced it.

"We maybe gone off-trail from where Heath and the Mexican will come back," he said. "But not too far, I reckon. If they happen along anywhere close to here, we got a chance. Say we fire off a shot every half-hour. If they ain't too far off, that'll fetch 'em here."

"I'd say we might be firing off a lot more than that," Christy said tonelessly. "Look."

Three figures on foot were coming across an undulating rise. They were still distant enough that the heat shimmer made their forms quivering and indistinct . . . but they were coming straight on the track. Christy sighted in her rifle, nestling her jaw along the stock.

Looking at her, Jason thought of how it had been

with them a few hours ago. Love's demand flaring in the face of danger; she guiding and patient with his awkwardness, bringing them both to the jet and joining of fulfillment; life's hunger reaching for the white-hot flowering that was life's essence, counterpointing death; these were precious things to have close in memory when the hot muzzles of death were seconds away. She's beautiful, he thought, the most beautiful thing I ever knew. Maybe I'm in love with her. Maybe I ought to say it.

But he didn't. Together they'd touched a moment of being that was isolated from past and present and future, shining and inviolable. Some vague intuition he couldn't begin to define told him that to speak of it, even at such a time as this, would destroy it.

Now the three men were coming into the long boulder field that faced the cliff, moving with the plodding tread of exhausted men. It took a lot of hate to flail men on like this, the kind of hate Val Penmark had felt. There would be no quarter given in this fight. And now they were moving faster, their gait lifting to a slow trot as they sized up the situation ahead of them. The tracks they followed led toward a natural fortress: even if they couldn't see their quarry yet, nothing could be plainer.

Jason settled his sights along the Winchester. "Hold your fire till I let go," he said quietly.

The men were coming into range, but taking advantage of the rock cover now, slipping along from one boulder to the next. Jason could get only glimpses of them, but the approach would be harder for them to manage as they got closer. His hands began to sweat, and he dried them carefully on his shirt, one at a time. He shut down coldly on a grain of panic.

You got your own rifle, he thought; you know what it can do. Don't worry about that. Just worry about what happens if they get to you and her.

Trask Ermine was ahead of the others, picking out their way as he loped in a bent-over run from one rock to another. His gangling movements had a kind of deadly rhythm so that Jason began to gauge when each short run would come. As he got nearer, he would get careful, Jason thought. Why wait?

As Trask ducked from sight once more, Jason sighted quickly along the edge of that rock. When the outlaw lifted up to run again, Jason led him just a trifle, then pulled trigger. Trask went spinning under the slug's impact and dropped in a cluster of low rocks.

Both Pete and Cherokee came scrambling out of shelter to reach Trask's side. Christy's rifle opened up with Jason's, echoes of gun-roar clapping across the rock field. But in seconds the two were out of sight, unhit, down beside Trask on the ground.

"Anyhow," Christy exulted, "that fixes the big one. You fixed him, Buster!"

Jason shook his head. "Winged him. Not much of a hit either."

"How could you tell?"

"You know, that's all. You get the feel of a shot and you know."

"Oh Lord—Jason! Look at that! Look—"

A band of riders were streaming darkly across the brow of the heat-shimmered rise. They were coming at a furious run, so that in matter of seconds Jason could make them out as Apaches.

The Ermines and the half-breed had seen them too. They came piling out of the rocks now, Pete supporting his brother, stumbling up along the incline toward Jason's and Christy's position. Making a desperate scramble for safety that was heedless of the guns before them—of everything but the danger pouring up on their rear.

Christy looked wildly at Jason. "What do we do?"

"Let 'em come," he muttered. "It's their only chance. And maybe ours . . ."

From behind these rock breastworks, he was thinking, five guns could stand off the Apaches. And maybe they could come to terms with the Ermines after. But even as the thought came, he knew with a chill certainty it wasn't going to happen that way.

Savagely and recklessly quirting their ponies through the rocks, the hostiles were already overtaking the three men. The Ermines had fallen well behind Cherokee; they were still a hundred yards from the cliff. Forced to turn at bay now, they began shooting. The Apaches had opened fire too, but they couldn't pull much of an aim from running horses.

Jason opened up at them, and so did Christy. Caught by their fire or the Ermines', two of three hostiles in the lead went spilling from their ponies. Then Pete

Ermine was hit; his great bulk folded to the ground.

The third Apache came thundering down on Trask Ermine, his lance set. Trask had pulled himself erect to meet the charge, but apparently his rifle had jammed. He flung it aside now, palming up his pistol. His left hand fanned the hammer in a racketing roar of shots as the lance left the Apache's hand.

The hostile was crumpling sideways as he raced past, then fell headlong from his pony. And Trask Ermine was toppling backward, the lance projecting from his chest.

Cherokee kept coming in a weaving low-bent run toward the breastwork of rocks. Jason tried to give him a covering fire, levering and shooting as fast as he could. Pulled up short by the fates of their comrades, the other Apaches were already off their ponies and scrambling for cover. They weren't slow in returning fire.

Cherokee was two hundred feet from the breast-works when a bullet broke his ankle. He plunged down. Floundering to his hands and one knee, he started to crawl, his useless leg dragging. He hadn't gotten three yards when a second bullet slammed into the back of his head.

"Oh God," whispered Christy.

"Hold 'em," Jason said hoarsely. "Space your shots. Got to reload. . . ."

Hurriedly he refilled his magazine, swearing as the Winchester's hot barrel singed his hands. He tore the bandanna from his neck and wrapped it around his left hand. Christy levered and fired steadily.

"Hold your fire," he said. "They've quit—hold it! Don't waste any shots!"

Silence settled across the baking scape. Jason's heart thundered against his ribs. The shocking toll of these few savage minutes left him shaken—but not shaking. He was steady, Christ, he was steady in spite of everything—or because of it.

The Apaches opened fire again in a desultory way. Some of the slugs came close, whining off the rocks. Twice bullets came so near that Jason felt the sting of flying chips. Yet he judged that by keeping low and using ammunition sparingly, they could hold this position indefinitely against the dozen or so braves.

Some of the Apaches now undertook to work in a little, rock to rock, but they'd gotten nearly as far as they might without becoming the open targets Cherokee had been. That last hundred yards was the crucial distance. Even if they made a concerted rush, two repeating rifles would cut them down like wheat stalks.

It was another standoff. Only worse.

He wondered what had pulled this band onto them in such a fury, swarming to the attack like wolves dogging a bleeding deer. From all he'd heard of Apaches, that wasn't their fighting style. It didn't make much difference, except that the odds against survival had taken an abrupt hike, like moving from a frying pan to hell's hottest fire. The hostiles wouldn't give up, not after losing a couple men. Jason did not hope anymore, except to see that neither Christy nor he were taken alive.

Several of the Apaches appeared to be holding a caucus of some kind. Afterward a pair of them went fading back through the rocks. Having an uneasy inkling of what they might be about, Jason shifted part of his attention to a tall promontory off to his and Christy's right. If a couple of men were to circle and get up on that, they'd have a far better angle of fire. And once that happened, it could all be over very suddenly.

"What're they up to?" Christy asked.

"I reckon they mean to get up on that side place yonder. I'll tend to that. You watch in front of us."

Minutes later he caught a hint of movement at the top of the promontory. A man had crawled on his belly to its rim. Jason flattened down against the shielding rocks as the shot came. It made a screaming ricochet that was way to his left, but the brave wouldn't be long in correcting his aim.

Jason shot back as another rifle opened up beside the first, shrouding the rim with powder smoke.

One of the Apaches below began to sneak nearer under the covering fire. He was a giant of a man Jason had sized as the leader, and he made a quick weaving run just as Christy fired. His body jerked to the slug's impact just as he reached another rock, plunging down behind it.

The two on the rim laid down a blistering fire at the breastworks now. Jason and Christy hugged the rocks. Then Jason felt a numbing slam in his leg. He twisted his head till he could see the spreading darkness on his pants. No pain yet.

The rifle fire slacked off briefly. Christy saw he was hit; she began to crawl to him, and Jason waved her furiously back.

"That one in front you nicked," he said. "We got to get him. Him first of all. You got that?"

She nodded.

He'd remembered one of Pa's hands, an old Mexican, telling him that if a war chief was killed, it turned an Indian's medicine bad and spoiled his belly for fighting. It was something to fix on anyhow. Right now, what else did they have?

Another burst of cover fire from above. As Jason had hoped, the big brave made another reckless move, maybe to pull his men into a charge. He sprang up to sprint for another rock. But he was lurching with his wound; it slowed him fatally.

Jason's bullet twisted him in mid-stride. And then Christy's shot drove him back into the rocks.

A yell went up from the Apaches.

One of the braves on the rim leaped to his feet, taking aim. Before Jason could swing to cover him, another rifle spoke. The shot's brittle echoes still pounded as the Apache pitched outward, his body crashing down the face of the promontory, tearing loose an avalanche of rubble before it came to a stop.

Hope surged in Jason the same moment that a hot flare of pain hit his leg. "Someone," he said between his teeth. "Someone . . ."

Someone. A sudden ally, No—more than one. Now two rifles were banging away from a hidden position.

In a moment Jason placed it as being somewhere on the cliff above Christy and him, but well to their left, two guns sweeping the rock field with steady fire.

Their positions almost entirely exposed to that fire, the Apaches broke into swift retreat, pausing long enough to gather up the bodies of their dead. A pair of them ran a risky gamut to race out and snatch up their fallen leader. Then they were gone, fading like brown ghosts among the rocks. So had the remaining Apache on the rim.

The clatter of their ponies' hoofs sounded briefly and then dwindled away in a maze of canyons to the south.

XVI

Their saviors were Heath and Miguel. Returning from the ranch of Miguel's cousin with the horses they had purchased, the two had been some distance away when the shooting began. They'd lost no time in getting to this place and seeking a vantage point from which they could determine what was going on. That vantage was the sandstone rise at whose base Jason and Christy were forted up. Coming up on its other side, Heath and Miguel had been too late to help the Ermines and Cherokee, whose bodies they could see among the rocks. But it had been clear from the way the Apaches were directing their fire beneath the over-hang that they had an additional quarry cornered.

Nonplussed as they'd been by the situation, it had seemed a time to shoot first and ask questions later.

After driving the Apaches off, Heath and Miguel circled down to the base of the rise, where they found Christy looking to Jason's wounded leg. Trask Ermine was dead, but his brother Pete was alive, shot in the side but not seriously. He'd played possum after the Apache bullet had brought him down. It hadn't even penetrated his ribs, having lodged in the hard fat that sheathed his thick body.

After sending Miguel to bring the horses up, Heath listened to Christy tell what had happened. While she talked, she tended Jason's leg. It was a clean wound; the bullet had passed through the outer flesh of his thigh, and both openings had bled freely. After washing it, she put on a tight bandage.

"Well, well," Heath said idly. "Seems you folks have been up the mountain and down again since we saw you last. But you fell into a piece of luck after all."

Jason sat with his back against a rock, his leg straight out before him. Watching Heath's face as he casually lighted a cheroot, he had an uneasy feeling that his own luck hadn't taken much of a turn for the better. Christy was on her knees beside him tying the bandage, and now she looked up at Heath.

" 'Luck,' " she said bitterly. "I don't know what you call lucky, Jack. Dallas is dead. He died helping me. Or doesn't that part of it ring any kind of bell with you?"

Heath flipped the match away. "Of course it does. Dallas was a friend and comrade. We'll treasure his memory and all that, eh? But this is no time to be holding post-mortems, my dear. . . ."

Pete Ermine glowered at them all. He was sitting in the overhang shade a few yards away, his shirt off, holding it wadded over his side. "One o' you might lend me a hand," he growled, " 'less'n you aim to leave me bleed to death."

"Well now, Pete," Heath said easily, pleasantly, "can you think of a good reason we just shouldn't?"

"Look, I didn't mean your woman no harm. It was Trask was all hellfire to run these two down. We just went along, Cherokee 'n me. Wasn't nothing else we could do."

"Is that right?"

"Sure. Way I figured, Clayt ast for it. Why, he—"

"Shut your lying mouth, you fat bastard. I've a mind to finish the job on you myself."

"Jack—" Christy got to her feet, and her voice held a quiet plea. "Hasn't there been enough killing? Look, let me plug that hole in his side, and we'll send him on his way."

Heath eyed her with a cold irony. "You seem to relish playing the devil's advocate, Christine. Funny, but I've the feeling we've been through all this before. That damned forgiving nature of yours has a way of slipping us into jackpots."

"Oh?" she said acidly. "You mean like talking you into keeping Jason here alive and well? Listen, mister, if he hadn't been alive and well back at Arrowhead Tanks, I might not be now. Or doesn't that ring much of a bell either?"

"Steady down, angel."

"Look, what's to be served by more bloodshed? There's all the money if you want it—his and Trask's and Cherokee's—and I'd imagine they took Dallas's share off his body; you'll likely find it on one of 'em. Give Pete a horse, some grub and water, and let him go. He's lost two brothers, and nothing to show for it but empty pockets and a chunk of lead in him he'll have to ride a long way to find someone to dig out. That ought to satisfy even your twenty-carat sense of justice."

Heath showed a dry and unpleasant smile. "Well, our little rustic Portia. You do argue your cases admirably, my sweet."

Miguel came up, leading the string of a dozen horses. They were tied together in pairs to a long rope with three-inch rings secured to it at eight-foot intervals; the horses' six-foot halters were attached to the rings. The Mexican said wryly, "I don't think we need so many horses, huh?"

"Seems not," Heath said. "We'll take the lot of 'em along and get rid of 'em in Sonora. We'll be moving without delay . . . those damned Apaches might be back."

"Ha, I don' think so, *jefe*. I see this one big Apach' is kill, they take his body away. I see him once before. That was Cayetano himself. With him kill', they don' fight no more for long time, I'm think."

"Well, now that's fine. The way is open to the border and we're all but home."

"Ha. W'at about these?" Miguel motioned at Jason,

then at Pete Ermine. "W'at we do with 'em?"

"Leave 'em a horse apiece and let 'em go their ways." Heath glanced at Christy, adding dryly, "That satisfy you, angel?"

"Drum's been shot in the leg, Jack. He's in no shape to ride."

"That's too bad. I'm keeping my word to let him go. I can't heal his leg for him. And we're not waiting."

"Nobody's asking you to."

"Now," Heath said gently, "just what the hell does that mean?"

"It means I'm not going to just leave him like this."

"I can make out all right," Jason said. "Ain't all that much of a hurt."

Heath ignored him, eyeing the girl steadily. "Been through a lot together, you and this lad, eh?"

"He saved my life. That ought to mean something to you."

"Why yes. Naturally it does. I'm just wondering how much it means to you."

Christy's jaw hardened. "You can think whatever you damn please. I told you how it is."

Heath flicked ash from his cheroot. "Did you?" he murmured. "Everything, eh? Now I wonder. It might not be significant, but I noticed when you mentioned the different shares of money, you neglected to take note of Clayt Ermine's share. An oversight?"

"No," Christy said quietly. "Jason has Clayt's share. He took it off his body."

"And you weren't going to mention it. But I'd find

out, wouldn't I, when I searched the bodies and found a share missing?"

"Just what are you trying to say, Jack?"

"What I'm saying, my sweet," Heath said harshly, "is that you're with me or you're not with me. Which is it?"

"Jack, listen . . . don't make it hard for me. You and Miguel can go on, I can meet you later, just say where. Can't we let it go at that?"

Not taking his eyes off her, Heath dropped his cheroot, grinding it under his heel with a controlled violence. "Why no. A few things need to be settled first."

Jason's rifle was resting on his good leg, and he had his hands flexed around it, tensed for anything. No matter what, he thought with dismal stubbornness, he wasn't giving up that money. Heath would have to kill him to get it.

"I'll tell you what we're going to do," Heath said.

"*Jefe—*"

Miguel spoke in a quick, sharply warning tone, and he was looking off toward the west rise of land. Two riders were coming into sight across it, moving briskly and coming straight on toward them. All of them waited, just watching now.

Jason felt the heavy slugging of his own pulse. Were these allies or enemies? Just be ready, he thought, for anything.

The high shape of one rider was familiar even before Jason recognized him. Val Penmark. Alive. And right beside him rode the Mexican girl they had left at Corazon.

"Sangre de Cristo!" Miguel whispered.

"Well," Heath said gently. "Well."

He lifted his Colt from its holster and gave the cylinder a turn. Then he held the gun at his side, waiting. Nobody else said anything, nor did anyone move.

A swarm of questions mingled with Jason's bewildered amazement, but the answers would have to wait. The next few minutes would write an answer of their own, deadly and final.

Penmark reined up, handling his horse left-handed as he quartered the animal slowly around to face them. Holding the Sharps rifle in his right hand, he stepped to the ground, not changing from a direct front to Jack Heath. He walked slowly forward and halted some yards away. His stubble-bearded face had a battered and drawn look, but it was as grimly indomitable as ever. His raw-rimmed eyes took in all of them, and then he looked only at Heath.

"Well, old pot. Came a long way for it, didn't you?"

"A blamed long way, sonny. I'll give you the move. Don't keep me waiting."

The Mexican girl slipped to the ground now. Still holding her own horse, she picked up the halter rein that Penmark had dropped and pulled both animals and the packhorse off to the side. Miguel too was shifting carefully sideways, hauling his string of horses out of line.

"I think we're in a stand-off right here, old fellow," Heath said idly. "Hadn't we better—"

Penmark was holding the Sharps across his body; he cocked it in one swift, savage motion. "Here and now. Make your move. Or I'll kill you where you stand."

Jason had his rifle up, and now, in plain warning, he let its muzzle follow Miguel's movements. The Mexican looked at him and shook his head. "I don' wan' in this. Not unless you say, *jefe*."

"No." A strained smile twitched the corners of Heath's mouth. "No, stay out of it—"

His hand cocked the pistol as he whipped it up, a steely blur of motion that ended in the flat crash of the shot.

Penmark was rocked backward, but then his legs braced hard; the heavy boom of his Sharps mingled with the blast of Heath's second shot. Heath was smashed clear off his feet, his body hurled backward. He landed loose as a flung and broken doll, and then he was motionless.

Penmark was folding down on his knees, the light dying from his eyes even before he slid over on his side. Just that suddenly, it was done with.

Christy dropped down beside Heath. "Jack. Oh God, Jack. . . ."

Miguel moved to Heath's other side and bent down by him. *"Santa Maria,"* he said, shaking his head. Then he tramped over to Penmark, thrust a foot against his shoulder, and turned him on his back. Heath's two shots had taken him in the chest in a space a man could cover with his hand.

Miguel looked at Jason. "Me, I'm think that's all. She's finish now. You think so?"

Jason nodded. The tension loosened from his belly and left him with a scoured and hollow feeling.

The Mexican girl walked slowly to Penmark's body, looking down at it. Her face was empty, showing nothing at all; and just as slowly then, she turned away.

Jason stared up at the black speck of a buzzard riding the white-blue sky. Even as he watched, a second bird coasted into sight. They always know, he thought dully. It was incredible how quickly they always knew.

The shadows of a waning afternoon stretched like gaunt fingers across the rock field when the burying was done. The broad common grave was packed with rock and marked by a rough cairn of more rocks. Yet anyone not knowing that it marked the last resting place of five men might pass it by without a second look. It was like part of the raw and tumbled landscape of its setting.

Jason stood with the others by the grave, holding his weight off his wounded leg. Miguel had done him the favor of searing both openings of the wound with hot iron. It had been excruciating as hell, and now the leg felt pretty stiff. But the pain was bearable, and he didn't figure to let it keep him down. He thought of Penmark's iron-bottomed toughness, and somehow it seemed a tribute to the man's memory not to let a knife scratch or fleshing by a bullet put him down—leastways not yet.

The girl 'Nita Cortinas knelt by the grave and prayed silently. After a minute she rose and, still looking downward, spoke quietly in her own language.

Miguel glanced at Jason; he lifted one shoulder in fractional shrug. "She say the old gringo, he would of take her to his home. She would of live' there and go school, she say. You think this old man, he do that for her?"

Jason shook his head. "I don't know. Maybe he would of. I didn't know him all that well."

Maybe, he thought, just maybe Penmark had found a reason to live before he died. It seemed better to think he had.

"Well, it don' matter no more." Miguel shuffled a palm cross his black-whiskered jaw. "Goddom, she's fonny how things go som'time, huh? The *jefe,* now he's gone it's like the whole game she's gone bad. I dunno, maybe it's jus' Miguel is getting old. But I'm think I give up the trail now. Eduardo my cousin, he's tell me that's what I'm should do."

Christy gave a slight, dull nod. "I know what you mean. I feel kind of that way. Who knows . . . it might even last."

"Huh. Look, you and the kid here, the girl and Pete too, maybe you like come to my cousin's with me. She's not far away and we got plent' horses, huh?" Miguel rasped out a dry chuckle. "You all be welcome there, you want to rest up awhile."

"I guess that's not a bad idea."

Jason nodded; Pete Ermine grunted a surly assent. "*Bueno.* Then we get going while the light is good.

221

Maybe we get there after dark som'time. You think you sit a horse all right, Drum?"

"I'll manage," said Jason. "Just one thing."

"Huh?"

"That money you people took. It's going back to New Hope. All of it."

"You wan' to fight me on that, huh?"

"No," Jason said flatly. "But I will." He glanced at the last of the Ermines, but Pete didn't even meet his eyes.

"Ahhh!" Miguel made a wry face; he swung his arm in a chopping gesture. "She ain' worth the fight. Som' money though, she's go to pay for these horse. I don' think you get that back. But you argue that with Eduardo. Me, I don' fight no more."

They all started toward the horses. Jason and Christy moved slowly behind the others, she giving him the support of her shoulder and arm. There was something he wanted to tell her, had to tell her, and it had to be soon. But how to say it?

He made a lame beginning, "There's something I want to say. I dunno just how."

Christy halted and looked at him quizzically. Then she stepped away, turning a little to face him. "Maybe you just better say it, Jason."

"Well, you know, I was thinking we done pretty good together, you and me."

"Were you?" His face got warm under her clear-eyed look. "Or should I say, did we?"

"Uh, well, you know what I mean. Fighting the Apaches and all."

222

"Uh-uh. Well, I wouldn't call that the Lord's way of pointing to anything better."

"I don't just mean that," he said stubbornly. "There's more, Christy—"

"Don't," she broke in gently. "Don't even try to say it, Jason. It would never work with us."

"There ain't all that much difference as I see it. What it comes down to is maybe you're five or six years older than me, but—"

"Five or six years?" A curious little smile touched her mouth. "Oh honey, I'm a hundred years older. Older than you'll ever be. Don't you know that?"

He turned his face down, a hard tightness in his throat. "I guess not. I don't know much. That's all right, you wouldn't want no green kid anyway."

"Jason. . . ."

Looking up now, he saw a tenderness in her face "You're every bit as much man as I ever met. Sometime you'll meet a woman, your own kind of woman, and then you'll think back on today and of me, and you'll know I was right. But I'll remember you asked, honey. I'll always remember and be grateful."

He jerked a nod, swallowing with difficulty. "I won't never forget you. Only . . . where will you go now?"

"Don't you fret about me. I'll make out. I always have." She hesitated. "There's a thing you might do for someone, though—I mean that Cortinas girl. Your friend Penmark made her a promise. It would be kind of nice if you kept it for him. I don't know how your people would feel, but she's a good girl, a decent girl.

223

That way, anyhow, she'd be their kind. It would be a fine thing for you and them to do for her. If you could see your way to it."

"Maybe," he said. "I don't know. Maybe we could do that."

"Hey," Miguel called. "Hey you two, come along. We got a ways to ride before she's get dark. . . ."

As they rode away and the sound of the horses faded, the wind stirred up a furl of dust. It sifted across the rock cairn and over the tracks, effacing the other signs of man's short stay. Soon their last traces would be gone, taken into the desert's workings. As it had for ages, only the timeless face of the desert would endure.

Center Point Publishing
600 Brooks Road ● PO Box 1
Thorndike ME 04986-0001 USA

(207) 568-3717

**US & Canada:
1 800 929-9108**